CONTENTS

The Terminated Abortion

When his wife Pragya gave birth to a second daughter within two years of their marriage Sohan and Pragya became worried.

They knew that Sohan's parents wanted a grand son. Only a grand son opens the gates of heaven for them once they die—they said, and will continue the name of their family.

The latter a grand daughter could not do, as she had to take up the name of the family she is married-off into. No one could confirm however, about opening of the gates of heaven, on account of the birth of a boy in a family, for his departed grand-parents.

These days some of the women retain the family name of their parents as well, along with that of their husband's, after their marriage. They typically have two second names after their first, like Sumita 'Pradhan' 'Manandhar', or Rasika 'Joshi' 'Adhikari', or Mira 'Pandey' 'Tripathi'.

It happens more often if the marriage is not arranged and instead is a 'love-marriage' – where the boy and the girl themselves select their life partner, with or without the approval of their parents.

Such marriages are noticeable and become a matter of discussion among the people, as they may cross the limits of caste or even community, at times, and are considered an act of rebellion against the practices in the society. More so if they occur in a small town like the one Sohan lived in.

Obviously, they may not entail a ritual donation of a 'kanya' (a virgin girl) as in an arranged marriage, to a groom, selected after gathering enough information about him second-hand; along with a dowry.

Parents painstakingly collect dowry to marry-off their daughter to a decent man who is educated, employed, and pliant enough to submit to the wishes of his elders in the family, to accept an arranged marriage.

At times they do so begrudgingly because they have to make a sacrifice of giving up many of their comforts and hobbies to save money for an attractive dowry for their daughter all their lives.

Someone with a son instead of a daughter is free of it. To find a suitable match for a marriage is an industry which employs many people, and sustains a few newspapers too, those that publish thousands of such advertisements in a special supplement every week-end. Those newspapers and jobs could disappear if most of the people here went for a 'love-marriage'.

As if the element of 'love' remains absent in an arranged marriage and choosing one's mate, as in a 'love-marriage' is a gurantee of an everlasting love in a marriage.

Some couples elope at times in a love-marriage, saving everybody in the society the rituals of kanya-donation, to later return to the family of the boy, where they are generally accepted back with a little remorse. But in some societies both the elopers are killed for dishonoring the name of their families if they belong to different religion or tribes.

The newspapers, including the ones that survive on arranging marriages, term such murders as "honor-killing", in which often no one is convicted, for the lack of a witness or evidence.

The women having two family names after their first name are considered modern and emancipated. Yet, there are people, not fully convinced of this type of women's-lib, expressed in their double second-names, like Sohan's parents, want to have at least one grandson to continue their family's name after them.

When everybody in the family dropped hints to Pragya in this regard and asked her to bear one more child, Sohan tried to protest, at times. Pragya always restrained her husband saying that this is how the society was. She was amazed to find that the women in the society were the most concerned or critical of her for not mothering a son.

So, within a few years after the birth of her second daughter, Pragya was pregnant again. Though she looked emaciated and fatigued due to the frequent pregnancies and the stress of child-rearing, she was unable to resist the pressure of her in-laws, and other elderly relations.

Now, since she was pregnant again, the pressure on Pragya was immense to bear a son. To release it she used to scold her two daughters, who have started to go to the school by now, for being unlucky to her, and asserted that this time it finally would be a son – who would bring her luck. Her elder daughter ignored her arguments as she had begun to understand the matters a little but her younger daughter appeared more concerned for her mother's well-being.

Pragya was properly, ritually-donated by her parents to her husband with an adequate dowry, through an arranged marriage. She thought she would live happily ever-after, as Sohan worked as a clerk in a department of the government, as it was a job for life, with a pension at the end of it. Besides Sohan's parents he had a brother who was more than a decade younger to him. It was a small family to manage for Pragya.

Pragya was expected to fit into the role of a traditional housewife for life, never mind the university degree she had earned. In most cases such degrees for women were an additional qualification to get married-off into a putative and well-to-do family, like a good dowry. Joining the workforce to earn a living was still considered not very reputable for a married woman.

After giving birth to two daughters things turned out very differently than Pragya had expected.

She was very worried if it was once again a daughter developing in her womb, as was every one else in the family.

Sohan found out that in the neighbouring town on the other side of the border – which was next to the Pragya's parents' village – a private hospital offered a service which detected the sex of a child not yet born through the 'video X-ray'. Abortion service was also available there which was still illegal on this side of the border in Nepal.

Also, no questions were asked there about the legitimacy of the pregnancy which was being aborted. So, most of the unwanted pregnancies were terminated there. If a couple from Nepal were seen at that hospital everyone knew that they are there for an abortion.

In fact Sohan has read in the newspapers that most of the women in jails of Nepal were convicted of receiving an abortion and were mostly from poor families, as if the affluent people never had unwanted pregnancies.

Not a single man was ever reported to have been booked for causing a pregnancy which needed a termination. Neither a doctor, who performed it, was ever apprehended. It appeared if becoming pregnant was the sole mistake of a woman from a poor family in this country.

Some people in Sohan's town offered abortion services clandestinely. They were called *Sudeni* and were not well-trained however and often landed their patients into problems.

Sohan remembered it well that his neighbiur's young wife died a few years ago soon after receiving an abortion during her third pregnancy from a *Sudeni* – leaving her two young daughters motherless.

That incident attracted the attention of the authorities as well. Somehow, Sohan's neighbour managed to avoid any serious inquest. People said that it did cost him dearly, to bribe the police and the health department officials, and rendered him a destitute.

The loss of his wife was too much for him to bear, and he could never get on with his life afterwards. He even declined a few proposals he received for his second marriage.

Soon he and his daughters left the town with very little money left with them. These days one hears that his daughters have turned to prostitution while he went insane and found a refuge in a mental asylum in the capital.

Sohan was worried if he was again going to have a daughter. On the insistence of his father finally he decided that they should find out the sex of the baby beforehand, even if they would decide about the abortion later.

He took Pragya to the hospital in the bordering Indian town. The doctor, after the 'video X-ray', confirmed that it was once again a girl, and, if at all, Pragya would have to undertake the abortion immediately, as later the risk would increase for her.

Sohan and Pragya felt very dejected at this news. They talked about how disappointed Sohan's parents would feel on this news. They decided that they should abort the foetus. Sohan asked the doctor to admit Pragya in the hospital for terminating her pregnancy the next day, before he went alone to the hotel where they were staying in.

During the night the thoughts of his neighbour's wife, who had died after receiving the abortion, came to Sohan repeatedly.

He loved his wife very much, and now became worried for her, in case if the abortion went wrong. After all, she was physically weak due to the frequent pregnancies and the emotional burden of bearing two girls. An abortion could prove dangerous for her.

He could not sleep the whole night. By the next morning he had made his decision. He went early to the hospital and told the doctors that his wife will not undergo the abortion.

The doctor and the other staff at the hospital were surprised and tried to convince him to let the abortion take place, as earlier planned. They even agreed to reduce the fees. They reminded him that if he came later, for the abortion, it would be late and will be more expensive and risky.

Sohan remained adamant on his decision, however; overruling the protests of a confused Pragya. He was very angry with his parents for keeping him under pressure to father a son which had endangered the life of his wife now.

They returned home in a rejected mood. Sohan's parents were totally unhappy at the turn of events. They scolded Sohan for not allowing the abortion to take place.

Sohan was not in a mood of reconciliation with his parents on this matter anymore. He told them that his wife would not risk undergoing an abortion, even if it was a third daughter.

He also told them that, she would not bear a child anymore. Also, if they were so interested in having a grandson, they could have their second son married. Maybe, his wife will give them their grandson.

His younger brother had grown up by now and had joined the army as a soldier recently.

Sohan remained indifferent when his parents told him that people marry many times in the society, if they do not have a son. He thought himself a modern man, and was happy with his daughters. He wondered why he remained so much under pressure to have a son, earlier, from his parents or other relations.

His parents stopped persuading him anymore to get his wife receive the abortion. They instead started accusing Sohan's wife of bewitching their son, and for taking him away from their control. They often ended by blaming their Karma for all these developments.

The days passed slowly. No one now talked about the pregnancy of Pragya in the family anymore. The undercurrents of the disagreement in the family were palpable however, even to the casual visitors.

Sohan's parents discussed in length the issue of their expected third granddaughter with almost everyone, at the slightest provocation. They lamented if they would be denied the entry into the heaven after their death, if they did not see the face of a grandson in their lives.

Some visitors empathized with Sohan's parents, while others privately congratulated Sohan and his wife for sticking to their resolution. Every day was an emotional high and low for everyone in the family.

Pragya lost her cool at times, as her inwardly festering hysteria broke. She too cursed her karma for her plight. At times, in presence of her parents-in-law, she needlessly beat her daughters – as if they were guilty for being born as girls – and then wept alone in repentance. She wanted to shift their attention away from her somehow.

In her heart, however, she was grateful to Sohan, for supporting her, and did not care much about the rest. Secretly, she and Sohan had made plans to go to a distant city, and build their lives separately, after the birth of their third girl.

Finally she had the labour pain and was taken to the health-post of the town where a trained nurse delivered the babies. The nurse was an expert and had a record of delivering upside down or obliquely placed babies successfully.

Pragya's delivery occurred without any complication however. Though there was a surprise for everyone: She delivered a boy.

Sohan's father was exhilarated by this news. He asked one of his neighbours, the one who kept a double-barrelled gun, to fire his gun into the air for five times, to celebrate the occasion – assuring him that he will pay for the cartridges later.

Pragya suddenly became a respectable lady for everyone, for delivering a son. Her daughters were surprised at the reception their brother received on his arrival.

Sohan, however, was shocked at the turn of events. He was dismayed to recall that they had nearly aborted the son his wife has now delivered; about which everyone felt so proud in his family.

He guessed that, in that private hospital, on the other side of the border, probably most of the pregnancies got terminated, to make the money.

Since abortion was illegal here, no one could complain about it later. He thanked god that, even unknowingly, he made the correct decision and saved his son.

The Harsh Priest and Mourning

The thirteen days' mandatory confinement for my brother and me, along with our stepmother and her mentally invalid son, to mourn the death of my father – who died when my brother and I were not around – was a unique experience. Sad though it was, it was also a chance to look at the world afresh without the protection and guidance of my father.

My cousins too happened to be there. The cousins were on their way back to Kathmandu, after completing the final rites of their own father – the youngest brother of my father – who died nearly three weeks before, in almost the similar circumstances, on the day before Shivratri; when all his children were away from him.

I was regretful though, and have remained ever since so, for not being around when my father possibly wanted me the most. It was actually the next day of Holi Festival, and my brother, who too lives in Kathmandu, like me and our cousins, was on the way home, on learning about our father's sickness. I sent him to see how serious it was the day we got the information. He was held up on the way by the disturbed transportation due to Holi Festival. He reached home around late morning, while my father breathed his last around one am. It must have been lonely to depart while one's children were not around.

My idea was if our father's sickness was not too serious my brother would take care of him, and if it was very serious he would call me as well. On learning about his death I began my two days' bus journey to reach home. On reaching home I found that the rest of the family had already gone to confinement.

I joined them after shaving my face and head, and the eyebrows. I was not supposed to eat anything on the way while I was returning. But I had biscuits, fruits and tea, as fasting during thirty hours' continuous bus-journey was not possible.

During the night of my journey I was very sad and often in tears. The next morning I met an old friend who keeps a shop in the town where my journey broke before I crossed the border to take another bus to reach home.

When he asked the reason of my sudden journey home, I could not explain, as I was in tears again. When I told him finally he consoled me with kind words and called up a mutual friend with a motorbike, to make my border crossing easier. Otherwise it entailed thrice changing a rickshaw after bargaining the cost with their pullers, or to walk for a mile with the luggage, if the gates of the bridge on the border were closed.

As they always were closed except during one hour each in the morning, day and evening. In between they were only to be opened for a government's vehicle of either side, though the waiting vehicles or rickshaws too were allowed to pass, along with a passing government vehicle. An ambulance too is allowed to pass at any time but not other vehicles.

The people in the government and the outsiders are clearly reminded of their standing in the system on the gates of this border bridge, built by the British colonials more than a century before. This still soundly functioning bridge testifies the solidity of the structures the British did construct. Not to mention the rigidity of the mentality of the people in the government. Which remains almost as colonial. Only the pedestrians or the motorcyclists could enter or exit through the narrower door at all times, but not a rickshaw, which a person on a long journey might use, to carry the luggage.

By the time I reached home I was in control of my emotions. I remembered that when I saw him last, nearly six months before, my father came to see me off in spite of my protests, holding the hand of my stepbrother.

I saw him waving goodbye on a poorly lit bus station, asking my stepbrother to do the same, as I left. I thought that would be the way I will always remember him – waving goodbye in half darkness; properly dressed, calm and dignified.

Though a little sad, which he mostly was whenever I went away so often in my life. He came every time to see me off at the bus station, at unearthly hours, when the long-distance buses mostly left.

However, I always wanted to stay back and be with him, but had to leave for my studies earlier and then for my job later. I wondered how he might have looked near his death when he was in pain. Fate denied me the opportunity to be a witness of that sight, and my father remained a stoic and composed character, in control of himself and always there to help me.

The attending doctor told us later that my father had developed an obstructive hernia and, given his heart-condition, was not a case to operate on, at the age of seventy-eight. It was not a consolation for me and I could not convince myself that nothing could have been done. When I said it to one of the friends of my father — who was near him when he died — if my father could have waited for a while for me and my brother; he laughed on it loudly. He said that it (the death) is like the wind blowing, which couldn't be stopped for anyone.

He further said that he asked the people around to let the body of my father remain in his bed till the morning, as the custom was to immediately remove a dead body from a house and keep it outside naked on the ground, covered with a piece of cloth. Someone was always attending it there till the funeral arrangements were made--to protect it from the scavengers or from touching by a passing animal.

It was something my father had said to me once--shocking me that a dead human body could be a food for the scavengers. My father's friend said that he always thought that even after death a person's body should be dealt with more respectfully than was the practice. For it had the life till a few moments ago which needed the comfort and protection of all kinds.

The thing I feared most while trying to make a living in the distant city had finally happened, and the sense of loss at the death of my father remains haunting till this day. I wonder what might have happened if I was around him at that time. Could I have arranged some better medical treatment for him, or said some kind words to lessen his pain?

"Punish your body son!" a friend of my father and our neighbour told me. "During these thirteen days of confinement and throughout the first year you mourn the death of your father you are supposed to lead an austere and a celibate life, denying your body any kind of physical pleasures and instead subjecting it to the daily rigours of a cold bath, prayer and other things!"

To one of my friends I protested: "How can I punish my body, as I love it? I never take cold-baths and never take more than two a week in winter."

Confinement for me was a period of contemplation. The days were filled with various rituals which also included listening to the 'Garud-Puran' in the afternoon after having a bath at a spring a little distance away from the town and offering prayers there in the morning.

My brother and I went to the spring barefoot with the priest and a friend, wrapped in white unstitched cloths and covering our faces with a veil so as not to allow any passer-by to look at our face. We knew that the people – mostly strangers – who came across us averted their faces at out sight, as it was considered inauspicious to meet mourners like us on a morning. That is why the people changed their way if they came to know that a route is being taken by mourners, for those thirteen-mornings, or waited till the mourners have returned for the day to be confined in their homes. A mourner could not leave home for these thirteen days for any other purpose.

The 'Garud-Puran' elucidates how the sinners are punished in the afterlife––telling in details how a particular type of sin is punished in what way and how an ideal life should be lived.

Our priest, who accompanied us to the spring every morning and performed the morning prayer there, read out to us from the book 'Garud-Puran' he produced from a bundle of books he always carried with him, wrapped in a piece of white-cloth. He translated Sanskrit into the local language.

On occasions we had to ask him to skip certain chapters if there was some other engagement more pressing at home, or we wanted to be silent and contemplative; or if the descriptions in the book became a little too violent, explicit or incomprehensible. On some days he was in a hurry himself, as he descended daily three miles downhill every day, to undertake these rituals at our home. By the afternoon he had to climb-back to his home on all those thirteen days. Tall and lean, he was fit like a long distance runner.

During this period he didn't accept even water to drink from our home, as everything after a death becomes impure till all the rituals have been performed to purify everything again. He also never ate a meal he did not cook. So he seldom ate anything away from his home.

He only had a big metal-glass full of tea provided by our neighbor after he finished reading Garud-Puran and was preparing to return home. It was the same neighbor who asked us to punish our body during the mourning period who gave him tea every day from his house.

He was our family priest and his ancestors undertook all the rituals for our family before him, be it a birth or a death. After him his sons were expected to do the same for our family. From him I got the first-hand account of the proceedings undertaken at the home of my uncle on his death– who was the youngest brother of my father. The priest undertook the similar rituals so recently for my cousins.

During this mourning period we ate only boiled rice with sugar and no salt. It was richly laced with ghee. We ate this meal only once a day. We had tea and fruits in the evenings. It was also a period of detoxification and I felt healthier and relaxed.

After food we expected the visitors to come. People came to express their condolence mostly on Tuesdays and Saturdays, which were considered inauspicious enough in our culture and just good enough to visit the mourners like us.

We were not supposed to touch or look at them

directly while talking to the visitors – and look sad at the death by not joking or laughing about anything. A white-cotton curtain separated us from the visitors and we folded inwardly the piece of similar cloth spread on the dried straws, serving as our bed, during those days, to avoid touching the visitors who were sitting on similarly inwardly-folded woolen blankets across the curtain.

They offered their condolence and discussed my father by mostly saying salutary things about him. At times some of them did it with exaggerations which looked insincere. Some visitors arrived early, as they were interested to listen to the 'Garud-Puran'. Mostly they were the elderly type.

Our grief appeared not as personal as I thought, as so many people came to share it. It was also indicative of the successful, worldly-way my father had lived his life. I felt deeply thankful to these people, for their kindness to share our grief. With some of our close friends, who were either classmates of our school days or neighbours, who also came to see us, my brother and I took the liberty to discuss the contemporary issues like politics. We even joked and laughed with them.

We became serious by hiding our smiles however, if someone not so well-known arrived in-between. A close friend and a police officer even accepted the tea we offered, which might have been sacrilegious for others to drink at our home before all the death rituals had been completed. 'But not for a policeman,' he said.

My stepmother, similarly mourning near us, hidden by a curtain from us as well, remained silent almost always. She cooked rice in the morning on a kerosene stove, which we all ate. She was not expected to go to the spring to offer prayers like us.

Every visitor brought fruits for us that lasted for many days after the confinement, and left some money to be donated to the priest at 'Godan'. 'Godan' or the donation of a cow to the priest, on the last day of the confinement, was the ritual which marked the end of the current rituals.

People said that before real cows were donated to a priest on such occasions. But nowadays priests accepted money in lieu, as carrying a real cow to a distant home of a priest could be a difficult process.

The mourners were supposed not to eat meat for one year afterwards, and I have stopped taking it altogether until this day. I became a vegetarian after my father's death. Alcohol however, I could avoid for only six months. I did not try, like other mourners, to wear white clothes only with no leather articles, for one whole year.

The mourners were also earlier supposed to refrain from having sex during this period. In some instances however, the wives of the people gave birth during or immediately at the end of the year during which they were mourning the death of a parent. Though they wore only white cloths and avoided touching leather articles during this period. Such matter invited ridicule of the society for some time, as it confirmed that the mourner could not abstain from sex during that period.

However, these instances did not linger much in the memories of the people. Nowadays the matters are mostly different as people use contraceptives so widely. In fact, people could be categorized in two groups: one those who were practicing birth control and the others who were not, due to varying reasons. Control of their fertility empowers people like nothing else. Its socio-economic and other consequences speak for themselves.

The sadness of losing my father was present in my thoughts during the confinement and later. I thought I will mourn his death for the rest of my life as well. I considered it useless to wear it on my face, to look miserable to satisfy the curious visitors.

However much the visitors tried to share our grief, it was at best only a formality. Or so I thought. I also noted that a few of the visitors hinted at how my father's property would be divided after our father, as they appeared to be on the side of my mentally invalid step-brother and my step-mother. I considered them as the type which tries to introduce disputes in a family. I politely informed them that we do not have much property left by our father to have differences over.

The thoughts of my childhood days often come to me even today. These memories are of both happy and sad times, when my father was always around with his reassuring words. I never forgot that he stopped using harsh words to my brother and me after our mother died early even when we had done something mischieveous.

His positive attitude was a great hope for me and the stories he told stimulated my imagination. It was during a time when only transistors were the only contact for one with the world beyond and the text books were the only books one read. His kind words during the time when I was sick or frail I still remember well. For they soothed my pain. Not getting a chance ever to reciprocate them was my biggest loss – as it appears to me even to this day.

It was on the thirteenth day after his death that we had to also finally make offerings to the '*katto khane bahun*'. A *katto khane bahun* is the priest who accepts the offerings which are made only after the death of a person and does not perform any other ritual.

Satisfying him was considered as equal to satisfying the departed soul. The priest was very demanding and he rejected all the offerings we had made, along with the money, telling us repeatedly that it was too little. He used harsh words to exhort my brother and me to donate more, in the name of our father. We were on the bank of the river behind our home, performing the ritual from the early morning.

The bank was half-lit by sun and rest was in the shadow of the tall mountain above the river. We had different articles laid out on the ground of grey-white, dry and slipping sand under our feet. In the dry sand every step one took went deep into the surface leaving behind an impression much bigger than one's foot. We were displaying to the priest what we were donating to him. Some food was being cooked in the lidless pans--which too were meant to be donated to him--seated on the spherical rocks found only on a riverbank, by a fire of woods under them.

We brothers were naked except the underwear we were wearing, and cold, due to the bath we had had in the river in the early morning before the ritual started. It was a late morning now but the sun has not reached there yet. It was a month of March and recently a new millennium has started and the air still had some residual chill of winter.

We wanted the *Katto Khane Bahun* to finish fast but he was stretching things to limits by arguing provocatively and lingering by making a fuss about everything.

We were anxious to return home and carry on with rest of the rituals with another priest who too was with us on the river bank along with our friend. In those rituals at our home our stepmother, who was not taking part in the present rituals, too had to participate, besides her son, who was waived-off most of the rituals, on account of his invalidity, but had his hairs shaved like us.

Only after a lot of bargaining and persuasion from us and our friend, who accompanied us always during our outings in the mourning period, and also from our family priest, that this priest relented, and accepted our offerings. Suddenly the things became quieter as we all fell silent, and the steady sound of the flowing water of the river became louder.

We returned home taking with us only the clothes we were wearing and a little cash we had saved from the *katto khane bahun.* My brother and I had a new sacred thread around our neck marking that our mourning was over by one more ritual – especially the one which was considered to be the most tyrannical one.

The rest of the things we took to the river bank now belonged to that *Katto Khanne Bahun.* It included many pans, pots, utensils, a mattress with a quilt and numerous other articles including various types of grains, spices, a small piece of gold and some cash.

We knew that, in future, we will not have to undergo such an experience again. Only after the death of a parent a son has to undertake this process. We will henceforth only have to offer prayers or '*sradha*' on the day our father died, as per the lunar calendar, every year, throughout our lives, after taking fast on the previous day. This is how our sons will remember us as well, after we too depart, never mind the daughters, who marry-off into another family, and observe the rituals for the late people of it.

The riverbank was in the glare of sun now. Its sand glittered with star-like fine particles. From the height we were climbing to return home, I looked back and saw the *Katto Khane bahun* and his two assistants who were still there on the river bank.

The assistants, who were supporting him while he was arguing with us – were actually his sons, I came to know later. They were putting the donated articles in a big sack while he was smoking a cigarette, standing a little distance away, facing the river, with the cash safely in his pocket. The sand in the ground near them was marked with countless, restless and indiscreet footprints, as if a crowd had a stampede on it.

Rest of the sand on the bank had no footprints. It was a mark of the time we had had there with that priest. They did not bother to look up to us. I turned back and tried to catch up with my brother and our friend and the family priest, who have climbed far ahead of me.

It was a queer experience for me. With the grief in my heart I nearly lost my temper when the priest harangued at us, demanding for more offerings and there were fierce arguments with him.

It was an event which was full of drama and nearly went out of control, as the priest threatened to walk out on several occasions. Everything looks well-orchestrated and theatrical – in retrospect, as I too started later threatening him of walking out.

We both were well aware that a priest or a *jajman* cannot walk-out on each other once a religious ritual has started between them.

I came to know later that every time this is how this ritual proceeds, no matter how much or less the mourners donate to the "*Katto Khanne Bahun*". I was then angry and thought that after such a loss to me of my father, I deserved kinder words from others, including the priests. His harshness was very disappointing to me as it was the first time I had faced such a ritual and no one remembered to brief us about it in advance.

Now I realize that it was one of the deliberate traditions of our culture which is meant to force you out of mourning and get engaged in the worldly business of life.

Without that shocking behavior from that priest I might not have been able to become distracted from my sad mood at that point of the time. I never met that priest after that day. In fact, no one likes to meet such priests on any other occasion. Due to the kind of rituals they undertake the *"katto khane bahuns"* are ridiculed in the society. They are the regular type of brahmans, who — due to some adversity--lose their high caste, after once they accept to undertake this ritual for the first time: of accepting donations to appease the soul of a dead person.

This renders them and their sons ineligible to undertake any other type of rituals. Theirs' is a peculiar kind of attitude, of profiting from a death, which is often used as a simile to disparage the people with similar tendencies in the society.

I am thankful for the harsh words of that priest, nearly seven years later, as they were possibly what I needed at that time.

The Cleaning Girl at the Temple

Bela got married to Vivek during his fifteen days casual leave from his army job, where he got recruited two years ago, as their parents had arranged. Soon Vivek had to return to his duty at a far away place. Though he promised to return soon, Bela knew that he would not return for another six months at least. Barely out of her teens, she found her body craving to fulfill the newly awakened needs.

Getting up early to fetch water in a brass gagari: a pitcher, on her head – balanced on a ring made by folding a piece of cloth for its convex bottom, and another on her waist – from a spring near her village, for the household needs and for the cow, buffalo and two pregnant goats in the Goth of her house did not inspire her.

Then there were the days with no water, as an insane person from the village emptied whatever got collected during the night in the pit in the ground surrounded by trees, early in the morning, before anybody could stop him. He claimed that it was poisoned by an enemy and he had a duty to save the villagers.

Soon her father-in-law, who also was a retired soldier like many other elderly people in the village, after having breakfast of boiled beans or leftover rotis and milk took those animals from their home to a pasture outside the village, for grazing. Bela became busy preparing meals and cleaning with her mother-in-law. There was no one else in the family.

By evening there was nothing much to be done, as her father-in-law returned with the animals and they all had an early dinner and retired for the day after doing the remaining cleaning and other chores.

The water used for cleaning utensils was saved to be given to the livestock, apart from the leftover food, since ash was used and not any detergents to wash. Water was a scarce commodity there. Only in summer the rains replenished fast the pit which was the only source of it.

Her father-in-law's pension and the money sent by Vivek through money orders every month was enough for taking care of their limited needs.

They had abandoned the rigorous lifestyle of other villagers of late. They purchased their firewood instead of collecting it from a nearby jungle, and bought vegetables and spices instead of growing them in the farm.

They even employed laborers along with their gorus (bulls) to till the earth and do other jobs in their ancestral farm in the seasons crops were sawed or harvested. It yielded them some grains but not enough. So they purchased the grains too from a nearby town.

A few other families in the village also did the same who had a member working in army or in a company in a distant city, who sent some cash back home. Those families also drank tea two times a day and served it to the people who visited them.

The children of these families could be seen secretively buying eggs from the blacksmith's house situated at the end of the village. The eggs were equally secretively boiled or fried to be eaten in their homes, though the lingering smell of fried eggs in the neighbourhood betrayed the reality often, on an evening lit by candles or oil-lamps.

All the villagers were higher caste Brahmins and were only supposed to be either vegetarians or eat the meat of a – castrated or not – he-goat, but not the poultry products. The blacksmith alone in the village raised poultry and regularly made some money from the villagers – more than what he made from his obvious profession of a blacksmith. Based on his caste he did his jobs in which he had no competition from the higher caste people.

The people of the village, like others in the vicinity, were the descendents of one common ancestor, and were either brothers or cousins. They never inter married.

The girls born in the village were married off to a man belonging to a similar tribe in another village and had no more claims on their parents' society. About it though they longingly reminisced for the rest of their lives, calling it maiti (mother's home).

However, they paid rare visits to their maiti on a festival, or were visited by their brothers or cousins at their husbands' home, at least twice a year with some gifts.

It was during leisure that Bela was burdened by her recently awakened physical needs. She waited anxiously for her husband to return home – something she was now expected to do always till he retired.

Her mother-in-law tried to tell her, sensing the restlessness in her manners; since she also had undergone a similar lifestyle in her youth, that, this was how the life was for the women married to a soldier. She also told Bela that later she gave birth to many children. Out of those only Vivek survived to become an adult.

Motherhood kept her busy in the absence of her husband, she told Bela. They were talking on one of those leisurely evenings after the final meal of the day while her mother-in-law smoked a bidi without touching it with her lips and holding it between her index finger and thumb. It was to hide or extinguish it between her palms if some one interrupted them. Being a higher caste woman her mother-in-law was not supposed to smoke but she did.

'May be you should become a mother soon,' she suggested to Bela.

Bela was unsure of herself while she listened to her mother-in-law, while her tongue explored her upper molars and her mouth was open. It was to hide any expression coming on her face.

Suresh lived in the neighbouring house and was about to retire from his army job next year. He was on his last, yearly, two-month's leave this time. Over the years his wife had grown irritable, as she had almost single-handedly raised their four, now teenaged, children.

Their two daughters were waiting to be married off to men belonging to a same or different village in the neighbouring hills. They were looking for suitable grooms for them as soon they started menstruating but so far they had no luck. Suresh was worried that this was a responsibility he will have to fulfill as soon as he could.

His two sons--who had already dropped out from their schools--were waiting to be recruited in the army. But nowadays it was possible only if he could afford the bribe to ensure them being not rejected due to a flimsy medical problem like wax in their ears. Or they will have to find a lowly job in a distant city in a private company.

The parents of Suresh died soon after his marriage, which took place immediately after he got the job in the army, due to cholera. In the following years he was away most of the time on his duty. So it was his wife who looked after the children. She was a clever woman to have grown four children, as in most of the cases, like that of the Vivek's mother's, the women in the area could raise only a few of the children they gave birth to. Water was scarce and the water borne diseases claimed many children every summer.

She had recently stopped having her monthly periods. During her periods, earlier, she was considered impure to be touched by her husband and she did not cook or offer prayer at the village temple.

But once she stopped having periods the demand of sex from Suresh rendered her quarrelsome, in her small, thin frame. She declined often, leaving Suresh, on his leaves, enraged and frustrated. Had it been in the place Suresh was posted in his job, he might have found a prostitute to help himself. But there were no regular prostitutes in this area.

There were a few cleaning girls at a nearby temple. They were part time prostitutes and their place always remained crowded even during the day by the drunken, unemployed men. Often there broke out quarrels among them.

Also, being seen among that crowd near the place of a cleaning girl at the temple rendered the reputation of a man scandalous in the area, as almost every man knew another in that crowd.

Particularly more so for a man like Suresh, who

was about to retire from his army job and was looking for suitable grooms for his daughters getting involved in any scandal was more precarious.

The cleaning girls were referred to as god-girls, a euphemism for prostitutes. They were from destitute families of the area. The rich persons of the area purchased them from their families to donate them to a temple, to do the cleaning services. It was considered prestigious to make such donations to a temple, for a man of resource and influence.

For a few days now Suresh was paying attention to Bela who looked very young and innocent to him.

She was a surprise to him in his neighborhood, as she was not there when he came home on leave last year. There was something mysterious about the way she went around, with her long curly hair falling on her slender waist. Her large eyes on her beautiful face always shifted on the surroundings.

She did not cover her head with a *pallu* in modesty like the other married women of the village.

It left her mother-in-law worried for how long it would take her to learn this essential manner of a married woman. Bela too noticed the attention Suresh was paying her. She did not feel uneasy and stared back at him whenever they crossed ways.

One afternoon, when the in-laws of Bela were away, Suresh entered her house to find her alone. She was waiting and willing to explore his well built body and to give.

Soon it became a routine for them. On some afternoons Bela went away to fetch firewood in the jungle – something she did not do earlier – and found Suresh there waiting for her.

At times Bela left the door of her house unlocked during the night and Suresh came in noiselessly, while Bela's in-laws slept soundly in the adjoining room. He left just before the dawn was about to break.

One day his wife discovered him returning at that early hour. Suresh told her that he had a bad stomach and he visited the field often during the night, to relieve himself. His wife believed him.

Holidays of Suresh were over and he returned to his duty, satisfied by the wife of his third cousin and not his wife this time.

It was time when Vivek returned on his yearly, two-month long holidays. He found his wife cheerfully responsive during the nights. The diffidence during the intimate time which he found in her earlier, when they were recently married, was there no more.

He returned to his job after passing two months, which appeared a very short time to him. He promised before he went away to take away Bela with him the next time, if he found a proper room to hire for them to live in, away from the barracks, where he lived now on his job.

A few months later Suresh returned to the village permanently on retiring. He expected to draw a pension for the rest of his life and take his livestock to pasture every day like other retired villagers from the army.

Bela resumed her escapades with him with enthusiasm. She found that these experiences were only making her wanting for more. For some reason she has not conceived so far.

Often her mother-in-law lectured her on how difficult the life of a wife of a soldier is.

She wanted to convey it to Bela that she had to be contended with whatever time she had with her husband. She had no idea about the good time Bela was having even in the absence of Vivek. The moral questions occurred to Bela at times. But the physical need always silenced them for her.

Then Vivek returned on casual leaves. Bela, forbidding the advances of Suresh now, asked him to wait till Vivek returned. But one afternoon, when Bela was alone in her house, Suresh forced his way in spite of her half-hearted protests. Bela could not resist his warm kisses. Just as they were about to finish making love, they heard Vivek calling, who had returned earlier than expected from the nearby town, where he had gone to buy the goods of daily need.

The neighbours saw Suresh running in his underwear from the house of Vivek, holding his shirt and pants tight to his chest and entering his house.

Shouts, thumping and dragging sounds, and swearing were heard from both the houses that whole evening. Suresh's elder son, reportedly, asked him why he did so to a woman in the neighborhood when his mother was available at home.

Next morning people saw Bela leaving the village forever, with her modest belongings in a bag hanging from her shoulders. Nobody tried to talk to her and she too ignored the people she met on the way.

She returned to her widowed mother at her *maiti*. It was a village a day's walk away after climbing up and down several hills.

Her mother tried to protect and console her as best as she could in the following months, as Bela was her only daughter.

Soon however, the wives of her two brothers--who worked in jobs in far away cities and returned home for short leaves only unlike in an army job--became intolerant of Bela when they came to know why Bela was rejected by her husband.

Bela was not happy with her dishonorable life at her *maiti*, where she found everybody talking disparagingly behind her--about her. But she had nowhere else to go.

After sometime she heard the news that Vivek got married for the second time to a woman from one of the neighbouring villages, and was living without any problem with his cousin Suresh in the neighborhood.

She was almost forgotten of in that village. It was difficult for her to think if it was only her fault. But there was no one she could talk to, to explain the matters, as even her mother did not listen to what she said anymore.

Bela tried her best to contribute in the domestic chores at her *maiti*, in her attempt to be accepted as a part of her brothers' household. But she felt that she was being increasingly ridiculed by her sisters-in-law.

It was unlikely that someone would marry her again, given the bad name she carried now, of being a loose woman. Working as a cleaning girl at a temple for the rest of her life she considered even more dishonourable as an escape from her present life.

After a few years she eloped with a barber belonging to another community. He had established a well-running shop in a nearby town where cinema music played loudly all the day and there were big, colourful posters of movie-stars on the walls of the shop, besides the huge mirrors.

Bela had met him while she went to the town with a few women of her *maiti* and one of them gave her young son a haircut at that shop. The barber got so much fascinated by Bela that he asked her to come to his shop often. Bela went there a few times during the next few weeks. He sold away his well-running shop at a throw away price and eloped with Bela one day. It surprised many people in the town and those who knew Bela.

No one has ever heard of Bela since. People guess that either the barber treated her well or sold her to a brothel in a distant city After all he was from another community.

Desires

'I never thought my son would dump me into this hotel at my age, when I have broken my leg,' Mohan Lal said. 'I thought he was expanding the business, when he started building this hotel, but like the other works he does, this too he left incomplete.'

He belonged to the merchant-caste and owned a business of dealing in electric wires and equipment. His wife died young, when his only son Sandip had just started to go to school, though he was already into his middle age. He had married a woman who was a decade younger to him as he worked hard to establish a business from a very early age. Soon after Sandip's birth it became apparent that his wife had a fragile health.

He blamed the uncle who arranged his marriage for finding him an unhealthy though young wife. One winter she cought pneumonia and passed away during a night in her sleep. Mohan Lal was a widower at the age of forty.

Due to some reasons, he did not marry again and looked after Sandip and his business well. People said that it was because of his overwhelming wish to become a rich man. Some guessed that he loved his deceased wife a great deal.

After her death, however, Mohan Lal was often seen sitting on a stool in the front of his shop, when he was not busy at it, staring at a passing young woman. He turned his head to the other side following the moment of a woman he was looking at, wearing his boat-shaped, white cotton cap.

Behind the counter of his shop he sat staring at the half-naked pictures of female movie-stars in a popular cine magazine called Filmi-kaliyan. His close friends also knew that he regularly read the notoriously explicit porn literature in Hindi called *Mastram*, as they exchanged or shared this literature with him.

Mohan Lal bought *Mastram* from a railway station

when he went away to buy goods for his shop from a bigger town in the neighborhood. *Mastram* was typically sold at a newspaper stall at a railway station, where the seller produced it from under his seat when demanded by a customer. Once this literature was strongly denounced by even Mahatma Gandhi and it was a banned literature.

On the mornings of Mondays, when mostly the women, who took a darshan there, visited the famous temple of the town, Mohan Lal could be seen standing behind a woman in the queue. He was pressing his crotch on her bottom. Just before he was about to be at the head of the queue, he went away and again joined the tail of it, behind another women. His shop always opened late on Mondays—therefore. His friends tried their best to convince him to marry for the second time. However, it was all in vain, for money-making was Mohan Lal's real passion.

He indeed had made some fortune in the business, to demolish his ancestral house of mud and stones, to make a new one of concrete, brick and modern style. His shop had to be shifted to a nearby building he hired, during the time the construction took place.

His building after reconstruction looked oddly taller and distinct among the old buildings of traditional style in the neighborhood. His shop shifted back into the shutters in the ground floor of it, and he and his son started living in the first-floor of it, as in their old house.

He proudly and noisily pulled the shutters up in the morning and down in the evening, everyday, while other shop-owners fumbled with the wooden flakes of the doors of their shops, which collapsed on each other to open. He also bought a small plot of land near the highway, which went to the border of another country.

Thus, apart from his lonely life as a widower, he had had a fulfilling life—or so he thought, with all his energies and hopes directed at taking care of the business and his only, motherless son. He hoped that his business will steadily grow in his lifetime and Sandip will take over it to finally becoming rich enough to open an industry—making the electrical wires and equipment he traded in presently.

Sandip dropped-out from school in his teens, promising to help his father in the business. Afterwards he idled with his friends most of the time.

He rarely exercised his body due to laziness and the affection of his father has turned him into a stubborn boy. Mohan Lal had to often yield to his whimsies, once Sandip became adamant on them. He never lost his baby-fat and went on depositing on it as he grew older.

During one hot afternoon, when heat forced the people to close down their shops and life almost came to a stand still until the evening, on the black-pitched roads of the town bazaar, which radiated heat to make the vision amorphous, Sandip was noticed among a crowd being led away by their shirt-collars by the police, after collecting them from the huts of the red-light area near the town.

In fact, only Sandip was a face from that town on that day in that crowd, while rest of the people – of various colours and creed, wearing dresses and headgears of different significance: communal or tribal – were from various neighbouring towns and villages in both the countries. They expected to return home by the evening, after catching buses and changing trains. Which they finally did this time too, but only after they bribed their way out of the custody of the Nepal police.

It was a common scene for the people of the town where people knew each other well for many gernrations. The town offered good quality alcohol at reasonable prices and its red-light area was full of fair-skinned prostitutes from the hills. The curiosity a face from the town in such a crowd created remained a matter of discussion and ridicule for some time.

Prostitution was illegal here too, on this side of the border, or the laws about it were possibly ambiguous, as certain tribes practiced it as the only vocation. Many social organizations have attempted routinely to rehabilitate the prostitutes, often by imparting on them some skills to make a living by joining other professions.

However, the stigma of their former profession never left the prostitutes, and they could rarely be integrated respectfully into the society again. Thus most of them, sooner or later, returned to the oldest profession. It was said that unlike the rest of the socity they became happier if a daughter was born to them instead of a son.

Or, so the newspapers reported, by bringing out a story routinely about the plight of the prostitutes of the town. Such newspaper stories always resulted in creating the curiosity among the people about the prostitutes afresh, near and far, and also causing an increase in their circulation and sales. Reporting about the escalating incidences of pre or extra marital sex did the similar tricks for the newspapers — though they blamed it on the influence of western culture, while concluding these stories.

A Journalist wrote a juicy story about the proceedings after he went to visit the red-light area of the town in the guise of a customer. From there he instead came out with a scoop of heart-rending story of a particular, anonymous prostitute — to whom he paid for sex which he did not have. He chose her story over her body.

Such stories, which were mostly the same, readers received with a relish and were widely discussed by the people of the area. Even a person living hundreds of miles away on both the sides of the border, who had never been to that town, was aware of the red-light area called Gaganganj in that town, and of the ambience there--to describe it himself. So much so, some people referred to that town with the name of its red-light area only. Thus, notwithstanding the illegality of it, the red-light area and the prostitutes remained there. Nowadays there are comedy shows on the television in which at times male actors dressed as females try to humour the audience by miming the manners of a prostitute and referring to Gaganganj in the show.

Mohan Lal arranged the release of his son from the custody of the police. Alarmed, but not angry, he hurriedly also arranged his son's marriage to a woman from a well-off family from across the border. The families on this side, belonging to his caste and his class, came to know of what a spoilt man his son had become and refused to marry-off their daughter to him.

Marrying his only son to a woman from a destitute family – which could not afford a respectable dowry – was what Mohan Lal could not contemplate upon. He had made some fortune out of a very hard-working and parsimonious life, in which he had to restrict himself from partaking in most pleasures of life.

After his marriage Mohan Lal expected Sandip to father a few children and expand his business. It became apparent however, after waiting for a few years, that there will be no children out of the marriage of Sandip. To his surprise Sandip took this development very lightly. He had put on weight to the extent that the rickshaw-pullers of the town charged him extra – or so the people claimed – to carry him around in the town. He often alone occupied the uncomfortable and narrow seat of a cycle-rickshaw meant for two persons, while the emaciated puller of it peddled mustering strength from his bones on a hot afternoon—as was seen by people of the town.

Sandip even played for a few years the part of Kumbhkarna, in the drama of Ramlila, staged every autumn in the town. Kumbhakarna was the ever sleepy and hungry giant brother of the villain Ravana, who enters the scene briefly in the mythological drama, when he is awakened by Ravana, to fight a losing battle against the Lord Rama. Kumbhakarna gets soon killed by Lord Rama but he is remembered for his loyalty to his brother. The viewers cherish the comical scene he creates while being awakened from his slumber in Ramlila, by Ravana. Sandip played this part admirably and his pet-name became Kumbhakarna to his friends in the town.

Sandip then thought about building and running a hotel on the land his father has bought on the highway. When he asked for it he got the approval from his father and the money needed—instantly. Mohan Lal always went out of his way to help Sandip whenever he took interest in the business. So far however, he had been a disappointment to Mohan Lal, as he had not shown any aptitude for business.

A few projects which he undertook only incurred a loss, as Sandip often got distracted by something, to abandon a project midway.

But every time he took an interest in a project Mohan Lal became hopeful again. After nearly two years Mohan Lal found that the hotel has been built and had started to operate. He was delighted on this development.

Sandip had built the ground floor which had six rooms facing each other on the front and next to the small lobby, and there were three rooms adjoining the toilets, baths and kitchen on the backside.

A hand-pump in the back was there for the guests staying in those three cheap rooms, who were expected to manually pull their own water. The six rooms on the front did cost more and had running water in their attached toilets. Next to the hand-pump was the staircase which went up to the solid concrete flat roof which covered the whole structure.

Sandip also had built two operable deluxe rooms on the first floor before something distracted him and he stopped more construction. Those rooms had no additional facility to be called deluxe apart from the commodes in the toilet. The rooms on the ground floor had toilets that could only be squatted upon.

Sandip consoled his guests staying on the ground floor that using commodes caused constipation or prostrate problems to their users in the long run and defecating while squatting was healthier hence.

The upper floor also had two unfinished rooms with gaping spaces for windows and doors and electric wires precariously hunging out of their walls and ceilings. Sandip assured his guests that those wires were harmless, as they were not yet connected to the power supply. Those unfinished rooms were visible from the front of the building and made it look grotesque.

The rooms on the first floor opened to an enormous verandah — not visible from the front — where more construction was planned in the beginning. Cool wind could be enjoyed in the evenings on the verandah, under the night sky, sitting on plastic chairs and tables, along with the chilled beer the hotel served, after the oppressive heat of a summer day of the town.

A few buildings in the neighbourhood were any more elegantly built than the hotel of Sandip. So Mohan Lal, for the first time, felt happy for the job Sandip had done, though the cost of the construction ran twice than what Mohan Lal had expected in the beginning. Sandip was running the hotel which was full to the capacity on most days. Mohan Lal thought if Sandip now was prepared to take over the responsibilities of his business from him.

After sometime however, it again became apparent that Sandip was not very interested in hotel-business either. Some of the well-known prostitutes of the town were seen frequenting his hotel and its most of the staff were women. Sandip had kept a huge bed in the small lobby of the hotel. He rested on it on his big belly with his chin in his palms and talked to the receptionist or other women he had employed, laughing hilariously at everything they said. Or he simply stared at them, if they were busy doing something.

He did not mind the guests of the hotel sitting on the wooden, uncomfortable chairs with no cushions in the lobby, observing his activities. There was only a very old and decrepit-looking man employed there besides the women, who either washed or slept in a corner of the lobby, making noises suggesting chronic, untreated sinus problems.

The hotel of Sandip started being frequented by his like-minded friends of the town and a few other young business travellers as well, who were, like him, interested in pleasures frowned upon by the society. His friends rarely paid any money for what they ate or drank there and he charged very reasonably to his guests.

In fact, Sandip, as usual, was not even remotely interested in making money, though his mild, mocking and friendly manners had earned him some regular customers.

There were rumours that, Sandip, incapable of having sex himself, due to impotency or his obesity, invited his willing guests or his friends of the town to have sex with the some of the women staff, who were previously working as prostitutes in Gaganganj, and watched them.

A few of his friends reported him unsuccessfully trying to mount a woman himself, before he handed over her to others. The ex-prostitutes working at his hotel or the willing guests did not mind his sport. Therefore, the enterprise of hotel was only to fulfill the fantasies Sandip had in his head.

Mohan Lal soon became aware of the happenings at the hotel and intervened. He closed it altogether and gave the building on rent to a finance company based in India. However, after a few months, the company absconded with the deposits of the people. Mohan Lal too lost a few months' house-rent, which was due on that company.

This incident made Mohan Lal chary of giving his building on hire, unless he found a dependable tenant. For some time afterwards the building remained unoccupied. Then Mohan Lal yielded to the persuasions of his son, once again, and allowed him to restart the hotel.

In the meanwhile, many of Sandip's friends of the town have gotten dispersed and his regular customers of the hotel switched elsewhere, and the scandalous reputation of Sandip and his hotel faded in the memory of the people. Sandip decided to keep a low profile this time, and went about his business discreetly.

His hotel no more invited any scandals like before, though he still employed a few women there, who had ran away from their families in the hills, in the north – mainly due to poverty. They ended up working as prostitutes in the Gaganganj area of the town.

Being bailed out by Sandip, with an employment at his hotel, was more respectable for them than working as regular prostitutes which left them vulnerable to various kinds of abuses and extortion – mainly by the pimps and the police -- as the profession was illegal.

Sandip now only entertained a few of his old pals and a handful of his regular customers in his sport, who he thought would maintain the secrecy. It continued in this manner for sometime.

Sandip soon found that he was not interested in the hotel business anymore; as he has lost interest in the sport he played there. Losing interest in something he was doing, midway, was his wont and he was now trying to find if there were some other fantasies he had which will be exciting to fulfill.

When he was thinking of closing down the hotel, his father broke his leg one evening, after he slipped while trying to cross the busy road while he was returning after purchasing vegetables from the market.

It left him bed-ridden and more irritable than before. Sandip and his wife earlier tolerated Mohan Lal's irritable manners and grumbling, who often blamed them for not giving him a grandson. After he became bed-ridden Mohan Lal became too cantankerous to live with.

He discussed his problem with everybody who came to see him, at his home, much to the embarrassment of Sandip and his wife. His disappointment of Sandip was profound. He had tried to persuade Sandip throughout, as best as he could, to marry for the second time—to have a son and continue his family. He had already taken help of all of his relatives and the closest friends of Sandip, in this matter.

However, Sandip always scoffed at such a notion and continued with his own ways.

Sandip shifted him to live in the hotel, on the suggestion of his wife—himself totally abandoning it. He went daily to check with his father at the hotel in the biginning. Slowly his visits became very sporadic and the hotel business his father started to run from his bed.

'I am not sure if I will live to stand on my feet again. I never thought Sandip built this hotel to abandon me to die here. It was my own mistake that I did not marry for a second time, due to my affection towards my son.

'I thought he will have children after his marriage and shall look after my business well. But he has been an out and out loss,' said Mohan Lal, lying on his back, on the bed on which his son rested on his belly, in the lobby of the hotel.

He continuously stretched his another leg beside the plastered, broken one, talking to any person interested to listen to his problem, out of the guests at the hotel, or from the relations, who came to see him.

The plaster on his broken leg from knee down to the toes looked heavy and help of the servant was needed to replace it in the bed. He had not completely become bed-ridden though and walked on crutches once in a while, or when he needed to go to the toilet. He was aware of the threat of bed sores if he did not leave the bed.

But he needed the help of the servant, to do so. He had fired all the women employed by Sandip at the hotel. Only the old, decrepit servant was there now to look after him and the hotel.

The old, regular guests still mistakenly came to the hotel, thinking if still Sandip ran it. They were offered only the rooms by Mohan Lal, as even the kitchen of the hotel was closed now. Moahn Lal kept the accounts and collected payment now.

'If I live to stand on my feet again, I think — if not Sandip — I will certainly marry again. How can I see my family finishing like this? All the property I have earned with so much difficulty... What will happen to it? I cannot imagine my nephews enjoying it after Sandip.

'Even if I marry at my age, I know I am capable of fathering a child,' he said with particular emphasis, while he shouted simultaneously to hide his embarrassment for saying these words, for the servant to take away the crutches from near him, and stand them on the wall.

He put the smallest piece of Jilebi, broken from a bigger one, in his mouth, from a plate in front of him. He worked hard on that piece with his only surviving canine tooth and a few molars perhaps, on his lower jaw. His wrinkled, clean-shaven face under the unwashed white hairs distorted due to the effort, until he swallowed the piece finally.

The calm returned to his face, after the sudden turmoil of the effort. The age had rendered his face very small, like that of a young child — if one ignored the wrinkles around his lips and eyes. He spoke again then, after what appeared like a long time.

'You know a man has to hold himself till he can feel the woman pumping,' he tightened and loosened his clenched right fist a few times to elaborate. 'Only then he should release himself. Else a woman could not be made pregnant. I know it very well. Only if I live to stand on my feet again, I know what I need to do now.

'Never thought my son built this hotel to abandon me to die here,' he said again.

The old man sadly died a few months later, never able to stand on his feet again. Sandip went on to live the way he always did.

Blow Hot and Cold

(ONE)

This year it did not rain the way I had known it does in Kathmandu. In fact, on the morning of July 7, 1986, when I reached Kathmandu for the first time, hoping to start making a living here, the valley looked like a huge lake of dense fog from Thankot, after a fellow passenger hailed Lord Pashupatinath loudly; making the people around him awake, or, if they were not sleeping, distracted from their thoughts, and peep out of the window of the bus.

Later I was to learn that some of the people did so at Thankot, to thank the God for safely arriving into the city, negotiating all those treacherous roads through the hills, out of which many buses dropped into the River Trishuli, over the years, during the night, while most of their passengers were sleeping. The remains of some of those buses were never found, even by the divers called from the army of Bangladesh. Only a few bodies were recovered many miles down the stream, at a dam in India, a few days later, as the newspapers had reported. In rainy season the great volume of muddy water flowing just a
few meters below the road makes a fearfully-charming view. It reminds you of the mysteries of nature, which can create or destroy life at whim.

It was raining throughout, while I was traveling by a night-bus to the capital city; and by the trains through the plains in India the previous day, making exit at one point of Nepal to enter back at another, as there were no continuous road connections within Nepal to reach the Kathmandu then. Due to rain everything looked green and washed during the day. The silence of night was broken only by the sound of the bus-engine and rain, lit mostly by the headlights of the bus, which gaped into

nothing at a bend in the road – the two beams of powerful
lights. The occasional lightning in the sky also
illuminated the surroundings briefly, but only to make it
become more mysterious. You had a little idea about the
land you were passing through. By the relentless and
distinctive rattling of the rain on the bus, that you
felt the consternation for what lay ahead, in an
unfamiliar place and among the unknown people, to be
found at the end of the journey.

Finally the storm was over and the dawn broke
slowly, gradually making obvious the green surroundings
refreshed by rains, which changed their appearance by the
minutes, due to the increasing intensity of the light.
The mist was rising out of the woods near and far; and
the clouds in the sky gave way to the rays of sun to
spread their golden touch on some of the landscape in the
far away hills. The dawn revealed the reassuring beauty
of the land around, to bring hope to subside the fears of
heart, caused by a restless and stormy night.

When our bus entered the fog, while descending
into the Kathmandu valley, from Thankot – a point where
the climb is over while going either way – into Kathmandu
or away from it--by the late morning, we appeared going
deeper into a cloud, with nothing visible beyond a few
feet. The land was wet with heavy rains and the road was
underwater in some places.

It was only later, on my countless returns to the
valley, from the official tours, which took me away
almost every week, that I realized that, from Thankot, on
a clear day, the whole Kathmandu valley is clearly
visible with all its splendor: The snow-capped peaks of
Himalayas in the north, and hills green with forests on
all the other sides, in almost every season of the year.
And the landmarks like the Tower Dharhara, now crowded
increasingly over the years, by the haphazardly
constructed buildings of the city, and the Swayabhunath
Dome on top of a hillock, made a fascinating view. Even
aircrafts could be seen landing and taking-off from the
airport, like small toys, in the eastern horizon.

On the day I first arrived here this view remained

hidden from me due to the dense fog, and the city remained mysterious to me ever since. The view that I later got tired of, after climbing the tortuous, winding roads uphill, to reach Thankot countless times over the years. The hills which look so attractive otherwise are mysterious. They charm you by offering a different view when you pass them during your journey almost every moment. It could actually bewitch one to the extent that one could forget to notice the time before it has started to close on him.

The buildings of the city looked usual to me – I mean the ordinary residential buildings, which were not very different from the ones you found in smaller towns. Only a few were distinct due to their huge size or unusual design. I was later to learn that they were either a hotel or a government office, designed and erected mostly by the foreign builders.

Later, I was also to be educated about the architectural and cultural heritage Kathmandu Valley was, with its ancient villages hidden behind the modern looking surface of the city; and the mysterious temples or monasteries of those villages – with their old woodwork on windows or doors, still surviving intact after centuries – protecting either a fierce looking image of a deity, forbidden to be photographed, or a sacred image of the meditating Buddha, in metal or in stone, behind them.

There were equally mysterious people you found following a narrow lane, leading to an even narrower one, until it ends in a cul-de-sac, in your search of a village in the valley, which has survived the face-lift of modernity. The modernity: which is unconvincingly represented mostly by either the shopping malls full of Chinese goods of dubious quality, in the high-rise buildings with escalators and unnecessarily large glass windows; the buildings which may also be hosting a branch of an international bank, trading all the kinds of international currencies, for god knows what purposes; or the showrooms displaying the Korean automobiles of all hues and Japanese consumer durables, accepting credit cards for the payments. Evading this deceptive façade, you finally find the people living a life as ancient as the valley itself, who have never gone beyond a few kilometers from their homes. You might be lucky if you did not encounter a housewife sweeping away the dirt from her house's wooden balcony, having a floor of red mud; who is not minding the people walking in the lane below, who run to save their heads from the falling dirt, or from the similar emptying of dirty water from a house. Else you might also have had to run to save your head. The garlands of red-chilies and the bundles of garlic hanging from the outside-walls of a house, for drying throughout the winter, must have been there a century before too.

The refinement of the available monuments left a lot to be desired – as it appeared to me – though the symbols of heritage were there, almost everywhere. There was a nagging inconsistency in whatever was apparent, or the talks you had with the people. For example, there were Union Jacks made on the wall of the old Royal Place: Hanumandhoka, which were not visible under the white distemper to me, before one of my friends pointed them out, though I heard often that this country was never colonized. Once I went to Singhdurbar, from where the government of the country operates, but which was built as a residence for the hereditary Rana Prime Ministers of the country, the elegance of its construction and the decorations inside I found truly amazing. I recalled that half of this building was destroyed by fire nearly thirty years ago. My father said that the "nose" of Nepal had burnt down – with his propensity to use symbols to explain the things – while giving us the news he has heard over the Radio Nepal. I and my brother were in primary school then, and this news was of no importance to us--living so far away from the Kathmandu.

It was clear that certain prestige was attached to this building, by the people across the country, which was one of the most expensive and elegant ones, during the time it was built, in this part of the world. I was told very little of the locally available products were used in it. I tried to imagine how it might have looked with its grandeur, before it was damaged by fire nearly thirty years ago, among even poorer milieus around it, in the countryside or in the capital, with its long galleries, staircases of marble, and the carpets of Iranian make under the chandeliers from Belgium. However much you tried to grasp what you could not see but doubt is lurking beneath the surface, or symbols, remained ever elusive, in Kathmandu--as it appeared to me. For there were rumours as well, in the years that followed, that the Singhdurbar was conspiratorially damaged by the authorities themselves, to destroy certain files, which contained the documents proving the widespread corruption in the affairs of the state. So the ambiguity in the nature of the people is not totally unfounded, as they have their reasons to appear as cynical as they do.

During winter too, if you reached the Kathmandu valley in the morning, by a night bus, it remains similarly engulfed in the dense, cotton-like layers of fog. It is only during the day that the sun finally penetrates the valley, making the people warm for a few hours before the chill of the evening greets them.

The sun sets behind the tall hills of Chandragiri in the south-west in winter and a day turns into a night almost instantly at six pm-- with no trace of an evening. Just like an electric light is switched-off, the going down of the sun behind Chandragiri makes the Kathmandu valley suddenly dark.

During summer however, the evening extends up to seven-thirty pm. And the sun, like in the plains of the country, remains visible as a big orange-red globe that can be seen with naked eyes, as it has lost all its heat and light by then, before it is swallowed by the thin layers of cloud, or it sinks into a gap between mountains at Thankot.

On one occasion, a few-years ago, a solar eclipse was seen from Kathmandu on a such late-summer evening, harmlessly visible by the naked eyes, with a tiny black-dot of the moon slowly traversing the lower end of the giant red glob of the sun, taking more than an hour. It made a spectacular view.

So the weather and schedule of its day and night at Kathmandu have remained a puzzle to me, as have its culture and the people — though I have been living here ever since I came here first, and married a girl who rarely had been out of Kathmandu. My wife later explained me why the people of Kathmandu rarely leave the city. For them it is mostly not needed as it is the migrants who come here looking for job opportunities – like me. I considered it a common snobbishness of the people living in a capital city, everywhere. Because we had a migrant family from Kathmandu in the town I grew up, which had established a very successful business there. The native there had a similar snobbishness while dealing with that migrant family, which was very enterprising and had grown far richer than most native ones..

Just as you were about to make an opinion about something in Kathmandu you were surprised by something unprecedented and inexplicable happening. If you turned to the natives or *Raithanes* of Kathmandu for the answers to your puzzles, you always got arcane and incomprehensible utterances from them, which ignored your question totally. And you begin to wonder if the people here were as simple and spiritually-happy as they tried to look, and how much lurks behind what is apparent of them.

When your puzzles become riddles and mysteries, in exasperation, you turn to refer to the first day you arrived here, and then try to recall what went on in between — to try to make a sense of what is going on. But often you are at a loss.

However, after I changed jobs, my arrival at Thankot by bus was reduced to once in a month. It too became tormenting later, as I had my family, which I felt reluctant to leave behind, and too happy to come back to. The excitement of going to the places and meeting the people suddenly vanished from my priorities, almost as soon as I got married. I wonder now if at all I was as interested in people or places before also--or was just trying to fill in the emptiness I had in my life, without a family in Kathmandu--though I had my parents back home.

I visited them only once a year, or less often, if my job needed me to stay in Kathmandu. The world still remains open as ever but I rarely have felt the need to go out and see it the way I did before. I do not wish to conquer it anymore either, as I thought I could, when I was younger and more prone to consider myself powerful, wise and brave.

Thankfully more these days, I rarely have to travel out of the valley. If at all I go away, I go by air, saving me the climbing of the bends of the tortuous winding roads leading to Thankot, while returning. Air-traveling I like only because it turns a ten-hour bus journey into a ten-minute one, due to the hilly terrain of the country. For often another town to land in is just across the hills on the horizon.

I resent even those ten minutes in an aircraft, and feel good only when I have landed. My claustrophobia of the interiors makes me run for the door to leave the aeroplane as soon as it opens its door after landing. It irritates some people. But often most people are themselves in a hurry to leave the aircraft after it has landed.

It happened once while going to Simra. It was a twelve minutes' flight to substitute a nine hours bus journey. As soon the plane took-off it started making preparations to land, as Simra airport is just across the hills in the south of Kathmandu.

But the noise of the twelve-seater Twinotter aircraft of the state-owned Royal Nepal airlines was too much to bear for me, and I developed an ear-ache that brought tears to my eyes. I asked for water, which the airhostess said was unavailable. I struggled on landing and vomited on the tarmac while getting out of the plane, and collapsed on a bench in the waiting room at the Simra airport. I rested for an hour to recover. Then caught a rickshaw to reach the Birganj Town, as taxis did not operate there--then. A friend told me later that it happened because the plane was not pressurized. Whatever it was, but the short-journey, as short as that, proved a nightmare to me.

I rarely miss the world from which I return to my family. I feel happy to remain confined to the cocoon I think I have made around me, of my thoughts, habits and preoccupations, which I consider are so essential to me. Having run out of energy and courage to run into the unfamiliar, I had to come to terms with myself somehow: the person I thought I knew. Else the life would have been difficult or even impossible-- trying to fit into the impressions the people had of you--while also trying to build a mundane living out of an ordinary job and around my family and hobbies – too happy to meet only the people I really wanted to.

I once asked a German woman – a friend of my wife – what made her come to Nepal for the fifth time in a decade and go to places in Latin America, Spain and China, which she said she had also visited. When I suggested her that people and their hypocrisy is the same everywhere-- she just smiled and ignored my question. But one of her friends, who thought that she will live in Bangkok for the rest of her life, after she had retired, due to its warm weather, as she suffered from a disease that became worse in the cold weather of Germany--could live only for a few months in Bangkok. She was troubled by the sex-tourism of it and could not stay there long.

I think my living a crowded life by people has made me blind to the world beyond them. I just explore the people I come across, for what they are. Occasionally a tsunami or a Katrina makes me afraid, reminding me of the superior invisible power, which at one stroke destroys the world people so painstakingly try to build for them. I wonder if the worlds we build are so fragile that is it worth putting so much hope or faith in them.

I soon forget these thoughts and become obsessed with the people who influence my world--by crowding it mostly. For I have a nagging doubt from quite an early age that the my equity in the world is being eroded or stolen by unseen forces. That is how the system works seemingly. So, turning eyes from the more obvious in life would be a total loss, though there is a regular persuasion to do so, by those very forces that live off the equity they have stolen from others.

In fact, most of the modern education renders people with instincts of a hustler and ever short of finding ways, means or ideas to put up something of a genuine value. Reducing this waste of human efforts, due to the lack of corresponding rewards, is what the life could be all about – if there is a wish on the part of one who could see the whole design.

A teacher at a British primary school in Kathmandu commented once in an interview that, unlike in England, she has mostly seen here people reading the newspapers only. She worried profoundly for why the Nepalese people do not read a more serious literature. She probably had no idea that most of the people are worried here like me, about their eroding equity; and about which the newspapers drop a hint instantly—mostly by denials.

Ignoring newspapers to read a serious literature, to discover this fashion in a much nuanced language, is for the more assured kinds like the British teacher, who could also afford it as well. Notwithstanding their obsolescence elsewhere, the newspapers will remain in fashion here, for the foreseeable future, at the very least.

(TWO)

This year the weather at Kathmandu really surprised me. During the months of July and August, when the rains are the norm and bright days are exceptional, it happened just the other way round. We had very humid days with cloudless sky turning purple from indigo, due to the bright sunlight and the heat. If at all there were some shreds of clouds there, they turned bright-white like satin, the thin layers slipping over one another effortlessly, blinding you by their glare. Occasionally, there was a heavy rain to clear the pollution of the traffic, which, otherwise, reduces the visibility to the extent that, during the dry days of a spring or an autumn, the nearby hills – which always remain behind the clouds during monsoons – are barely visible as an outline, in Kathmandu. Even the Buddhist monastery Swayambhunath on top of the hillock is conspicuous only when it is lighted by electric lights in the night.

This year however, you could see the lush-green forests of the surrounding hills with clarity, as no clouds covered them and the dust was removed by occasional rains. If you used binoculars the scenes were breathtaking. In spite of the heat and humidity this year the charm of Kathmandu was on display, as usual, along with its culture.

As, on most days during a summer, a carnival slows the pace of the ever-busier-growing traffic briefly, when it passes through the main thoroughfares, after emerging from the narrowest of the lanes, before it reaches a temple with a fierce looking deity. Most of its participants are either blowing into or beating at centuries old musical instruments of various looks and make, while some of them try to put up a stumbling dance like performance, visibly under the influence of alcohol. The commitment of the people to their culture looks undeniable. They are out there just to indulge and celebrate.

Is this what that the German lady comes to see here so often? I remember that last summer she returned with a big wound on her forehead from Bhaktpur – one of the three towns that make the Kathmandu valley. She went there along with her Nepali boyfriend to stay for two days and participate in a carnival, or Jatra, as it is called here, which culminates by separating the people – most of them inebriated by alcohol – into two sides, which end up throwing stones at each other, while cursing in an abusive, obscene language. Many people around there sustained wound injuries and some had to be hospitalized, as happens every year—she told us.

I was not aware of that carnival until that day, taking place in Kathmandu; though I knew that a similar one took place in the remote hills of western Nepal every year. The German woman read all sorts of books and did the research to discover and participate in it and similar other jatras, while she was here. I cannot forget the happiness she had on her face while her wound was covered by a dressing which covered most of her forehead, when she visited us with her friend.

She was beaming when she told us that the police just watched from a distance, while the people threw stones at each other and shouted abuses, not interfering in the cultural celebrations; though they helped to dispatch the wounded people to the hospitals in the waiting ambulances.

(THREE)

The bright days always troubled my eyes. This year, before six am in the morning, my east-facing sleeping room was filled with an orange coloured sunlight that had no heat yet, penetrating the thin curtains of synthetic fabric, which my wife purchased in spite of my protests, as I always favoured heavy cotton ones in dark colours. The light was so intense that it was impossible to remain in the bed. Reluctantly as ever, I had to leave my bed to buy milk from a nearby grocery-shop, with my sunglasses on. Then I heated the milk for my sons and prepared tea for me and my wife; before waking them for another day. When they were up it was time for me to go away for my morning-walk. I returned tired and drenched in sweat, as if it was a walk on a hot afternoon.

My apartment gets the sunlight during the whole day, as it is on the top-floor of the house. So I had to wear my sunglasses always this summer, even while I was at home. Here people wear them only when they go out, but seldom at home. So, to many of the visitors, I had to explain my reason for wearing sunglasses right from the morning onwards in my home, or while going out.

I emphasised to them that I was not suffering from viral conjunctivitis--which becomes an epidemic here every summer, and forces the afflicted people to wear sun glass and use antibiotic eye-drops for about a week--but was sensitive to the sun-light. Lest they would not avoid shaking hands or making other bodily contacts with me, fearing the transmission of the virus.

Very few of them believed my explanation. They thought that I was becoming prone to fashions in my middle-age, taking inspiration from the white people of the expatriate community living in the area nearby, who could be seen jogging on the roads wearing sun-glasses, which were mostly of other than black in color, when it is barely a dawn. I did not mind that either.

After the day's heat my apartment became this summer really unbearably hot in the evenings. My south-facing kitchen-cum-drawing-room was particularly hot and it was not possible to sit there with more than half-pants on. During winter though, the same room becomes cozy and warm. I seriously thought about shifting the TV from the drawing room to my east-facing sleeping room, which becomes cooler in the evenings. Then I decided that I could do without TV-watching in the evenings, and read the newspapers instead, in my sleeping room; leaving it totally to my wife and children, in the hot drawing room.

Apart from the heat, the cockroaches, which infest my abode during the summer and hibernate there during the winter, were another nuisance that chased me away from the drawing room.

This year they seem to have flourished tremendously because of the heat and the humidity, and were out in the kitchen which is separated from the drawing room only by a waist-high counter, swarming and flying around, even before the lights were out. I did not have the courage to brave them to watch TV unlike my wife and children.

If you switched on the lights during the night, to find water; when the thirst caused by heat wakes you up often, you found brigades of the roaches there on the kitchen floor, walls and curtains. It was a mating time for them and they often forgot to creep as usual and instead took the aerial route, to find a mate—as it appeared. Sometimes they landed on you, if you fall in their flight path. Having them moving over your naked body parts leaves you wincing in agony. And you shake your limbs to get rid of them.

At times you mistakenly step on one of them and it bursts open with a sound you recognize, spilling the body fluids. But it was still not dead and runs away to a corner unsteadily, with its body parts coming out of its skin, leaving behind a trail of body fluid. Exasperated with a queasy feeling, you retreat to the sleeping-room hastily, shutting the door; and try to sleep, forgetting the sight. Earlier my wife used to become squeamish even at the sight of a cockroach. But now she has learnt to live with them and shakes them off her body, if they land on her – but with a mild scream, which turns into a smile later. My sons too display similar tolerant attitudes towards them.

Earlier I tried to get rid of them by using a red-coloured insecticide spread on a wet piece of bread. Many were killed but many more remained. I forgot that all the houses in our area are interconnected by sewage pipes for the roaches and it is a species that has survived the vagaries of times since millions of years, while witnessing even the dinosaurs disappear. I gave up the futile exercise of trying to see the last of roaches, also fearing that the insecticide could somehow contaminate our food, causing the trouble of another kind.

To my surprise, the small brown-coloured ants, which crowded the leftover food in our apartment in great numbers, have disappeared this year. Was it because of the heat and humidity? Or have the overgrown cockroaches devoured them? On occasions however, I have seen a multitude of those small ants taking on a fully-grown cockroach, which futilely jerked its body to shake them away; dismembering it body-part by body-part, while some ants ran away displaying a body-part of the roach many times bigger than their own size, to their hide.

In fact, until last year we did not have a refrigerator and stored the leftover food in a plate placed between another plate filled with water, to save the food from those ants. We then covered it with a plastic net, to save it from the roaches. Due to our newly acquired refrigerator our food remained protected and fresh this year. We also had the supply of chilled water to combat the heat and perspiration--thankfully.

This summer however, the supply of drinking water became a little scarcer than we were used to. We soon discovered that our neighbours have started using a two horse-power, Chinese-made electric pump, to suck the water out of the supply. While until last summer every household in the neighbourhood used a small, half-a-horse-power pump. Using that too was illegal, if one went by the rules. That tacit understanding among the neighbours, of using smaller pumps, was done away with this year, by the people who could afford the bigger pumps. Thus, while our house ran without drinking water on certain days, our neighbours had a plenty of it, which they displayed by washing their car in their compounds, almost every day of the week; with a pipe supplying the water in a generous stream. We could only watch this spectacle helplessly, with a few other owners of smaller-electric-pumps, like us, in the neibhborhood, as complaining was not possible to the authorities, since pumping water from the supply itself was illegal.

The authorities have devised an innovative policy of denying the denizens of Kathmandu a good night's sleep in summer by supplying the drinking water at around two am only, on alternate days. So one has no choice but to buy the water in a tanker once a week, or be ready with the paraphernalia of water-sucking from the supply on alternate days, at that early hour indeed. This year I noticed that on certain days the power supply disappeared during the time the water was supplied, rendering all the electric-pumps ineffective, irrespective of their horse-power; and the water getting distributed evenly. I thought that the government was genuinely trying to bring equality among the people.

Due to the scarcity of water, we had to use it many times to wash different things, before using it to flush the toilet. I permanently removed the lid of the flush in my bathroom to continuously fill it with the water we had saved after baths or washings.

(Four)

With the autumn ahead now, the chill is there in the morning air, and the demand of the water has reduced, as manifested by its improved supply. I have replaced the lid of the flush. But, until the month of December, the roaches will continue to roam around in our apartment.

The winter of Kathmandu is so cold that you forget if you ever had a summer here. It preoccupies you with its requirements so totally that you also forget that it will be summer again, by winter's end.

Hopefully, keeping in mind the hot summer this year, the winter ahead will be a mild one. No one can be sure what is in store to happen in Kathmandu, however. It is what I have learnt over the years.

Right into Left

(ONE)

"I support the right in my country and the left in the neighborhood or beyond..." This thought came to him clearly while he mentally was trying to avoid the smell of rotten egg his wife has just broken into the cake she wanted to make.

It was the sixth and the last egg to go and had a thin whitish liquid with no yolk when it was broken.

It filled instantly the kitchen with a nauseating smell. All the other ingredients like sugar, dry fruits etc have already gone into the pot.

The thought of throwing away it all was painful, though he suggested it to his wife. She confirmed his thoughts by insisting that they should go ahead by putting it in the oven and bake the cake. She was with a little success trying to remove the rotten egg's curd like white content from the paste already made, with the help of a long plastic spoon which also served as stirrer and whipper.

'Let us put some litchi squash in it, so that the children would not notice the bad smell,' Saroja said, while resuming stirring the contents in the pot. She had decided that more of that bad egg could not be removed from it.

Of the foul smell lingering in the morning air of their apartment, they were not sure if it was coming from the paste in the pot or from the sink where Saroja had dropped what she thought was the most of the rotten egg, after separating it from the paste.

It was a hot and humid morning. The thin rays of sun penetrating the sparsely spread dollops of cloud bore a promise of a yet another sultry day. Things already appeared going awry with a rotten egg getting mixed in the material for the cake.

"Yes, let us go ahead with it and mix the squash

in it," said Govinda.

Their children had already left for the school. "After we cook it we will see if it is fine or not. But next time make sure that you break the eggs separately, before mixing them with other things. Remember once you found a dead, decaying fetus of a chicken when you broke an egg to make an omelet?" asked Govinda.

"But how can you tell a good egg from a bad one, tell me?" Saroja asked in a querulous manner, recalling that it had happened when they had recently married nearly eighteen-years ago and felt nauseated thinking about the scene.

She had screamed on finding a decaying chicken's fetus of brown color when she broke the egg. It made Govinda come running from the bathroom, with his half-shaven face.

It was a memory, like so many others, which was always fresh to both of them. What a long and remarkable period it had been since then--she thought.

There were times when they thought that their marriage was not going to work, while at others their lives together looked full of only bliss. The intensity of their relationship left no room for a feeling somewhere in the middle. Getting to know each other helped, though it was not easy--Saroja also thought.

Particularly when a situation like the present crisis had arrived, and they had to take a combined decision to handle it. As were their nature, if the decision proved wrong they did not give a second thought before blaming the other for it, and if it proved right they both jumped to take the credit for it.

So being together was like walking on a razor's edge mostly. A development of cynicism too, towards each other, was inevitable, as was the need to ignore it. The children, jobs, and the uncertainty of life in general were good distractions, however, to keep them enough apart—for the episodes of intimacy often culminated in quarrels, where, once broken, neither of them appeared to be giving in and making up.

"For that you have to put the eggs in the water.

The one that sinks is good and the one that floats is bad, " replied Govinda.

"When you return home for lunch from your office, bake the cake in the oven for a full-half-an-hour. Since there is no power supply now, I am putting it in the refrigerator. In the hope that it will not deteriorate further," Saroja said, ignoring what he had said about eggs.

She was ever unconvinced of the wisdom and economizing ways of Govinda, which left most of the things he prepared only half-cooked. He often ate alone the half-cooked vegetables after preparing them himself, as no one else liked them. The children, on the matter of food, liked whatever Saroja cooked and were suspicious of everything Govinda prepared. His experiments in cooking often yielded unfamiliar kind of food to them.

Saroja thought often that Govinda would eat everything raw if he could. She strongly doubted that if the cake went wrong today Govinda will make her children eat the most of it.

"I told you already to get rid of it," said Govinda half-heartedly, "but let us hope that it tastes alright and no one falls sick," he said, trying to reconcile the antagonism they were feeling towards each other for a situation which had arrived inadvertently.

He hurriedly had his meal she had cooked then and left for his job on his motorbike, fearing that the traffic might have already thickened in the roads from Kupondole itself. Saroja went to her work on her scooter a little later, when the morning peak hour of traffic has passed.

Going all the way to Baluwatar will certainly prove harassment--Govinda thought. The roads were dug at many places for laying a fresh pipeline for water supply as Melamchi project was about to materialise. It was expected to bring to Kathmandu the water from river Melamchi through a massive project which was for two decades in construction now. The slowly moving traffic raised dust continousy and there was a permanent haze in the air on busy roads in the city most of the day. Most pedestrian and riders of motor bikes used masks to avoid the air pollution.

If it was not a summer day Govinda might have used a city bus to prove his sound sense of economy in terms of money, efforts and--given the traffic-time as well.

A ride in a city bus in Kathmandu in summer left one soaked in sweat due to the crowd nowadays. He reminisced about the days when he had first arrived into the city, a little more than twenty-five years before. He thought how open and pleasant the city was then.

When he boughted his first scooter its number plate confirmed that there were still less than twenty thousand two-wheelers in Kathmandu. When he went on it to visit the poultry farmers in the villages outside the ring-road, to sell them feed supplement of the company he worked for, the roads had open fields with flourishing green crops on either side, till he reached a village.

Nowadays those open spaces have completely disappeared and buildings built on increasingly smaller plots of land cover that land.

The city has spread out to make those villages a part of it. Also, now there are more than four hundred thousand two-wheelers in Kathmandu, as could be confirmed by their number-plates, with almost no increase in the length or area of the roads. The space in the valley is limited. There has been a similar rise in the number of cars.

Trying to get out of Kathamndu to those villages outside the ringroad on a bicycle, so charming in those days, in the hope to get fresh air to breathe, turns into a nightmarish experience now. Those roads are now crowded by tankers bringing water from those villages, where there still are natural springs which have drinkable water, to serve the demand of a nearly dry Kathmandu city. It is now a city of four million people which has put a great stress on facilities which remain the same like before.

Apart from the tankers--trucks that ferry the construction materials like sand or granites found near those villages crowd those roads. Besides in those villages itself the construction is taking place and many trucks are ferrying material from the city there.

There is always a thick traffic in the ring-road and the police have declared it a no-parking zone. The characters have become unlikely therefore, who went in a car to the ring-road, in a story of Samrat Upadhyay, to have unprotected sex--the consequences of which they suffer later after it results in a pregnancy--in it while it was parked in a lonely, abandoned area, covered by bushes or trees in the ring-road area. That scene has simply disappeared like most of the unwanted pregnancies.

At the Kupondole bridge the traffic was moving slowly as Govinda has feared. The local buses were lingering on the wrong lane near the pavement before they came into the right one, obstructing the way for the vehicles following, on either lanes.

Their cleaner boys were beating the body of the bus with their palms and shouting "Ratna park! ... Ratna park!!", still looking for the passengers, well past the bus stop.

Govinda remembered that during his Delhi visit last winter he saw some of the buses not having any cleaner boy or chaos, when they stopped or moved, except the rush of people during the peak hours boarding or leaving it.

They instead had a gentlemanly conductor, calmly sitting on his seat in the back. To him the people went to buy the tickets, fighting their way in the crowd which smelled of sweat even in the winter. The conductor failed to inform Govinda to get out when he reached the station he had to drop at. Since he was new in Delhi he had no idea about its various locations. He had asked the conductor to drop him at a particular bus stop and the conductor simply forgot to tell him when he reached that stop.

If it was not for a fellow passenger, who mockingly called him a 'truck' when Govinda boarded the crowded local bus with his two bags, who informed him that he was already a few stations past the one he had asked the conductor to drop him at, Govinda might have gone further away.

He recalled that--that passenger was trying to catch his attention a while ago too, possibly to convey him the similar message. He had ignored that, thinking that too as hostile--as his ridiculing comment on him by calling him a 'truck'. There were other passengers too, with one or two articles of luggage in the bus. After all everyone can not afford a taxi to carry his luggage in a city like Delhi which was so widely spread, to avoid riding a local bus--Govinda thought.

However, thanking that ridiculing but helpful passenger and cursing the gentlemanly conductor in his heart, he got down at the next stop.

There was nothing of the speed of the city, with which Delhi appeared to move, about the bus. Getting frustrated at its slow speed a person from the crowd had shouted earlier if the driver of it was a rickshaw-puller before. There was a roar of laughter on it from the crowd in the bus, though the bus-driver challenged that person by inviting him to come and drive instead. The bitter-sweet ways of Delhi people begin to charm Govinda.

When he discussed it with his friend and host in Delhi, later that evening, Govinda was informed that it was a bus of government's ownership. There were private buses also available, called Blue-line. But they were dangerous: for they vied for catching the passengers, even on the main roads. They were on the verge of being phased-out for they have been involved in too many accidents.

The forthcoming Common Wealth Games could become a pretext for the government to take them off the roads of Delhi forever—his host told. Govinda immediately decided to use those old-looking private buses, as they were so much like in Kathmandu. He was not surprised when the cleaner of a Blue-line bus provided him a ticket where he sat and collected the payment with the change ready to return, and was more anxious than him to drop him at his destination--to make room for the new passengers.

For a stranger in the city like him it was comforting to know that he will not go beyond his destination--to return to it by catching another bus. He considered it a bad news that the private buses will be phased out from Delhi. But the trend was such about almost everything, as he saw it.

The government was slowly and steadily encroaching in the space of private businesses, often to itself run them, or to hand them over to the people it favoured.

He found it in Bombay, where he went a few years ago, that there were no private buses operating and the government's department running city buses had its own police force too.

The city of Delhi had grown mush bigger than he remembered when he once came here two deacdes ago. He had heard that the pollution has reduced after the CNG vehicles were introduced in Delhi. But the first thing he looked for after arriving was the face mask he wore, while leaving his house in Kathmandu, in the pocket of the jacket he had kept in a bag.

The jacket, so much necessary in Kathmandu, he did not really need while travelling to Delhi during the day and when he reached there on that pleasant evening of the January day. So he had hept it in the bag.

His host informed him that the pollution in Delhi has worsened due to the construction activities taking place almost everywhere, as he too had noticed while approaching it.

Delhi was on an expansion project of its infrastructure as the preparation for the Common Wealth Games which were to take place just half a year later.

An Indian official had claimed that CWG will be grander than the Olympics China had organized a few summers back, as reported by a newspaper. Though the same newspaper also had reported the escalation in the cost by six times than estimated initially, of the CWG, due to the wide spread corruption and an inordinate delay in completion of the different projects.

He used a taxi to reach the place of his host. It over-charged him many times, as his host informed him later, whose house he found after wandering for sometime in the streets of a residential area, though the driver of the taxi claimed that he exactly knew the address, when he provided it to him.

But anyway, that is how the taxi drivers in a city are--Govinda thought. On his inquiring the driver could not confirm if the engine of his three-wheeler was a Japanese one made by Daihatsu, as the sound it made was not different from the Tuk-Tuk of Kathmandu--though he relentlessly kept on complaining how the preparations for the Common Wealth Games have made the traffic worse and the roads dangerous.

....

He returned home during lunch hours to relax a bit, as always, fighting his way back in the traffic, which got worse as the day progressed in Kathmandu.

His duties entailed field visits to the customers till late in the evening. But his afternoons were free. He was glad to find that the power-supply had resumed and he could send the e-mail he was writing on his desk top. The power cut in the morning was not scheduled and left him in a flux with his half-written, urgent email remaining undelivered.

He hoped that the Hotmail he was using had saved it as a draft. It was a relief that the people developing things like Hotmail--who is an Indian actually--are prudent enough to foresee the problems like power-shedding and find a remedy for it as well.

So it is not only the ineptitude which prevails around. But one could not ignore the fact that Sabir Bhatia, who had developed Hotmail, before he sold it to Microsoft company owned by of Bill Gates, in a multi-million dollar deal, did so while working in the USA.

Govinda took out the plastic pot with the material for the cake from the refrigerator and put it in the oven. He fixed the time at thirty minutes and switched on the button. The oven began to hum with an occasional screeching sound it had recently acquired, perhaps due to a loosened part of it.

Soon the smell of rotten egg began to fill the kitchen. He retreated to another room leaving the oven running.

While he waited for the beep of the oven to announce the finishing of baking, he took out a book of a British author he has abandoned several times before. Govinda tried to read it in spite of the smell of rotten eggs engulfing this room too, by the anxious minutes, opening the page turned at a corner where he had left before.

It was his wont to leave a book unfinished to return to it later, instead of abandoning it even when he found it uninteresting; while he began reading another one. No one knew what his frame of mind might be, at a given time, and every returning to a book could make him read it with a different perspective.

Which, at times, could bring to light newer insights about the book or the author; or about the life itself, to one.

Undermining the physical or intellectual labor put up while making them, would be inconsiderate, by entirely abandoning them--though all the books are not equally successful with a reader. The world might appear poorer minus each one of them—Govinda thought.

The British writer continued to defy his expectations though, and the gratuitous description of scenes and emotions continued. A critic friend of a young girl's writer father continued to persuade her to believe what he thought about her father in a very fluent language. She reluctantly appeared to have agreed with him, in spite of her initial incredulity of those thoughts, which the critic insisted she too had of her father.

And her war-veteran and a successful writer father leaves to the wilderness that surrounded their home, leaving behind his confused wife and a son, apart from his daughter to the critic and his wife, to what appeared like fighting and conquering the wilderness.

Being a writer he saw the future himself and not through the eyes of his children--the critic friend of the writer tried to convince his daughter, who had dropped out of her school in scandalous circumstances.

In the meanwhile the Londoner wife of the critic tries to make herself up for every time of the day. They both were the guests of the writer. It was all very smooth but very fluid. The seemingly accurate description of matters and emotions eluded any idea of the area where the story might lead to. He found his patience thinning again with the book.

Any writing which tries to give an idea of the people to them is always fraught with disaster, as disingenuousness and pretentiousness threaten to plague it. It was a work by and for the people with an immense amount of security and time, and with no concerns for the demands that daily life makes on the working people.

He dropped the book again and took out a tablet of tranquilizer and swallowed it, as the two he took the last night to sleep, he felt, had gone out of his systems. The restlessness and confusion, with which the day was proceeding and the banality of the literature, which he hoped would alleviate his mood—left him feeling more agitated.

Even at its half the book was more open-ended than any Govinda has ever read. If it was not for its excellent language, and the review he had read of the book, which has hinted that later the young girl and the critic have a sexual relationship, he might have never returned to the book—Govinda thought wryly.

The reading of the review of that book had robbed him of the only surprise the book possibly had – he thought. Nothing makes a reading more common than the lack of surprise in its plot – he also thought.

(TWO)

The smell of rotten eggs has thickened in this room too, and he hastened to switch off the oven which had already given several rounds of beeps, announcing the completion of thirty minutes it was set for.

Entering the kitchen Govinda held his breath for a while, as the foul smell was stronger here. His doubts were confirmed that the cake had gone wrong. He switched off the oven.

"...unless the left fortifies itself to resemble the right, like in China." he saw the words coming to him to complete the sentence occurring to him for so many days now. It made him feel elated.

It was not such a bad day after all--he thought, while taking out a tab of nicotine gum, which he had started using recently, hoping to replace his childhood habit of tobacco-chewing.

It was after he met a young man, Rakesh, barely into his thirties, but looking much older, sitting opposite him in a train, while returning from Mumbai, which he preferred to still call Bombay, that he tried to stop using tobacco. Rakesh had a scar from his chin to his collar-bone, and a twisted mouth on the right side. He made him realize that oral cancer is a real possibility for the tobacco-chewers. Govinda switched to the nicotine gum.

Tobacco he has been either chewing or smoking since his early age and his efforts to drop the habit at different stages lasted from a few days to a few years--leaving him ever more frustrated, whenever he returned to it. His increasing age has rendered him vulnerable to the damage tobacco causes--he discovered with a lot of grudge, as he could feel distinctly healthy while not taking tobacco.

He recalled that nowadays the packets of chewable tobacco had a warning on it with a drawing of a scorpion, instead of a crab, to stress that it could cause cancer. The authorities have made it mandatory, but only recently--to mention such warning in public interest on tobacco products.

However, the youngsters not using chewable tobacco seem to be in the minority. There were more smokers in his childhood days than tobacco-chewers.

Some of his friends, who came to the school in his town from the villages in the neighborhood had acquired the habit of smoking after they were asked by an elder from their family to bring him a cigarette after lighting it from the fire at the cooking place. In villeges he had seen that fire of woods was always heating the open pots of brass, copper or iron. The Aluminum or steel made pots begin to appear only later and were comparatively expensive initially, before their costs dropped considerably.

His friends smoked cheap cigarettes or bidis during the breaks at the school in the open area near it, which abounded with bushes and served as an open toilet.

Similar toilet for the girls was on the other side of the school. Govinda did not recall when he too picked up the habit of smoking. In those days smoking could be an acceptable habit for men, more a sign of coming of age, than a vice, and was not frowned upon as it is done presently.

But for the children in the town it was not acceptable and they were constantly reminded by their smoking-elders to not take up the habit.

At least not when they were not yet old enough. In fact, a man with an income and family was also expected to smoke, but not so, for the women. Women did it secretively, though.

Nowadays the number of smokers may be on a decline but the tobacco-chewers have grown remarkably, as it could be chewed secretively—without producing the smoke. Even women could be seen putting tobacco behind their lips, in a train or in a house.

Govinda remembered having seen a young woman in a train putting the tobacco she had rubbed with lime powder in her palm in her mouth and then a little of it in the mouth of her infant son, who was stubbornly asking her to buy him a toy from a vendor. She was casually smiling, for the fellow passengers were watching them. Some of them smiled too, when the child's face distorted due to the bitter taste of tobacco, while others looked distracted.

He also had noticed an old couple in another train he had traveled in, who shared the tobacco similarly rubbed in the palm by the man, after he blew the finer parts of it by clapping his palm with another hand, making other people in the compartment sneeze or cough. He also noticed that the neck around the collarbones of the woman was abnormally thick, and doubted if she had already developed a cancer due to the tobacco she used, with all the homely serenity on her face of a housewife.

Rakesh told him that he was an electronic engineer by education, but was thankfully doing a clerical job in a district Magistrate's office, where his extra income was much higher than his salary. He had passed his electronic engineering when it had recently come as a new discipline to India. However, it never occurred to him to find a job in the corporate sector, which was just beginning to manufacture the electronic appliances like computers and colored televisions then.

Once he failed to find a government job as an engineer in the telecommunication company of its ownership, he applied for the clerical one in another department of it.

Thankfully, he got one near his home in a district in Uttar Pardesh. It was actually during his engineering college days that a few senior friends forced him to start by tasting a few grains of Gutka, which was a mixture of betel nuts, tobacco and other scented materials.

Then gradually he became addicted to it and resorted to it more during the time he was unemployed, to release the anxiety. After he settled in the present job he was devouring up to forty pouches of Gutka everyday. It was after more than a decade that there grew a small spot on his gum of the lower jaw, on the right side, and the inflammation would not subside by medicines.

He went to a hospital and the biopsy confirmed that it was a cancer. He was then referred to the Tata memorial hospital of cancer in Bombay, where the operation took place. His whole lower jaw of the right side, and a part of the larynx, were removed. Bones and tissues were taken from his thighs to graft there. After the operation Rakesh found his body opened at so many places and connected to so many tubes that for the first time he felt the grief for ever starting taking the tobacco. He also was angry with his friends who initiated him forcefully, to Gutka. He looked agitated for the first time when he said so--as it looked to Govinda. The train was briskly making its way to its destination with the familiar clicking sound. Govinda looked out of window to avoid looking at Rakesh who had tears in his eyes.

Soon Rakesh found his composure, as the rancor in his talks against his friends was gone when he started narrating his remaing story. He ironically smiled when the vendors selling Gutka entered into the train compartment at a station, with the garlands of Gutka pouches in their colourful packing around their necks. They were also selling chewing-gums and candies.

The endless fertile plains of India were green with flourishing crops, and it was raining at many places the train passed through. Only occasionally this view was interrupted when the train slowed on approaching a station; or stopped for a while at another, to drop a few passengers to collect the newer.

In the central part of India it entered a higher plateau full of big rocks, where the bushes abounded, and the trees grew smaller, and the crops were absent mostly. The shepherds sporadically present in their colorful turbans and their women in the dresses of matching brightness were tending the herds of sheep, with a few occasional camels. Though their camels were much shorter than the ones Govinda had seen in a circus.

The presence of those shepahrds increased the charm of a land, which was so green in the monsoon-rains. It was difficult to imagine what the newspapers were reporting during the last few years that many farmers were committing suicide in this area, due to the crop failures on account of perennial draughts, while some others were joining a rebellion against the state.

The insatiable desire to look at the landscape and the people on it had to be put on hold, when their sight relaxed and coaxed, in combination with the rhythmic movement of the train, one to sleep. Or when it became dark.

To be confined to an express train for about forty-hours was like being on an aircraft. There was nothing more important than the journey itself, which you might allow to bother yourself. You make an informal kind of acquaintance with a few fellow passengers near you, listening to their stories and telling them your's, as only they are there to hold a talk to break the monotony.

The monotony was also occasionally lessened by listening to the Hindi melodious songs of yore, sung by the singers no more, like the one sung by Md. Raffi, Kishor Kumar or Mukesh--apart from the ones sung by Lata Mangeshkar, who recently had celebrated her eightieth birthday. Those songs were played by a fellow passenger on his mobile phone.

There is of course a new crop of singers who are quite popular among the youngsters. But every generation has perhaps its own favorite singers, which it will be always reluctant to change. However, those old songs are heard less often nowadays, for the generation is always changing. But when they are played they engross you totally--Govinda thought, humming the tunes being played.

Also as even the new, pirated copies of an award-winning and another best-selling books fail to engage you for long, which you bought for less than a hundred rupees each from a footpath shop of a posh area like Marine-drive of Bombay, though they had a much higher cost in dollars printed on their back--that the monotony becomes more pressing.

The only thing you admire about those books is the scrupulousness with which the pirates have copied them. They were as good as the originals. It was contrary to the image you had in your head of the book-pirates, on account of a previous copy you came across, of another award-winning book, which you considered a second-hand one but original, while purchasing it from a bookshop in the tourist district Thamel of Kathmandu.

Only when you begun reading it that you realize that it was a word-to-word retyped copy, by the pirates, who were not good editors at all. So, while you admire the labor they have undertaken to produce the pirated book, on possibly a large-scale, to make it profitable, you wondered also that they were easy to catch by the authorities, if at all they were keen on it--or literate enough.

You also wondered if those pirates have worked as hard in some other profession they could have made a fortune out of it: as even in India, English book reading population is still not very big; as only the award-winning, or similarly-hyped books could be found for sale, pirated copies or otherwise--which fail to engage you even on a forty-hour long train journey. You could not help but admire the book-pirates of Bombay, which is the prime city of India, after all.

Indeed, it could be only Bombay, which could produce a scrap-dealer traveling in the air-conditioned-class of the train, in which Govinda; though a corporate worker; was traveling--making an exception though, as the sleeper-class was over-booked, with it's a third of the cost.

It is in the AC class in a train only that the TT wishes you good-morning, while asking for your ticket to check; or a fellow-passenger scolds the steward, who forgot to bring him a towel; along with the bed sheet, pillow and blanket he provided. The passenger who also reminds you not to buy the paper-soaps, as there will be liquid soap available in the toilet--he assures. And you also have a feeling of privacy, as there are curtains to pull to make you invisible behind them on your berth, from the mostly Muslim co-passengers.

They often gathered in a group and one of them read a story from a book which others listened reverentially. It described a person who lived centuries ago in an Arabian city, and who was strong enough to take on a mad elephant physically. There was nothing much you could talk about with them; who spoke among them a language which was polite to the extent of sounding insincere; which someone said was the 'Lukhanawi' language. Any kind of straight talking could have been taken as an offense by them.

In the AC class there is no continuous traffic of the passengers getting on and off, from the stations where the train stopped, like in the sleeper class. But there was a crowd of waiters in dress, who were supplying food and drinks from the dining car, at an inflated cost. At times they were three of them, following each other closely, all of them selling tea or coffee from a big steel pot containing boiled water, mixed with milk and sugar, which they dropped through a tap at the bottom of the pot, into the tiny paper cups – just half-filling them.

The tiny paper cups already had the coffee powder, or a tea bag, which got barely drowned in the liquid.

So, it was over after just two or three sips. Govinda suggested to one of the tea-vendors that, earlier, the tea was available in a train in the big kulhars (cups made of clay) poured from a kettle. Over the years the size of the cup has reduced so much that in the future one may expect to find tea in a train in the small plastic containers, meant to administer medicine syrup to children, though its cost will continue to go up. He laughed on it.

The lunch you booked from the a waiter for fifty rupees they were selling at forty, soon after they delivered to you—your ordered one, on a tray.

And you were surprised by the presence of a larva of a worm on top of the lunch packet after you removed the aluminum foil. It was cooked along with it.

Feeling queasy and angry, you threw away the entire tray of food, after coming out of the compartment and finding a door, as the windows of the AC class are permanently closed. When asked for water along with the food, the waiters made you wait for half-an-hour, as one of them is selling bottled and aerated water drinks, kept in a bucket along with blocks of ice.

A passenger lost his cool on it, it was the one who had scolded earlier the attendant for not bringing him towel, and shouted at them to immediately bring the water. And they brought the water in glasses and jugs— pronto. Water is a commodity earlier said to be free but not so increasingly, nowadays.

The scrap-dealer claimed that he avoided traveling to Delhi by air. He was getting a ticket at a low price due to the competition among the--now so many of the--private airline companies operating.

He said, in that case, he would have to take a train from Delhi again, to reach his home in the Gonda district of Uttar Pardesh. In future, if his district had an airport, he will directly fly to it--he said with conviction. So one could make it big, even while dealing in scrap, in Bombay, one could conclude.

The scrap-dealer was coming home to help one of his brothers-in-law in the local elections, shortly taking place there, for a post in the village-panchayat he was contesting for. The scrap-dealer said that there is some politics in UP of its own type, (probably the money-and-muscle type, as the Indian English newspapers speculated in their editorials). But it was nothing like the on going Maoist-war of Nepal.

Govinda recalled that he had met another passenger some time ago, who was returning home to his village in Jhansi district of UP, to fight a legal case in which a jealous neighbor had trapped him into. He ran a mobile footpath stall selling fast food for the last thirty years in Bombay. He complained that police and criminals extort money from him regularly, to allow him ply his business illegally on a footpath in a posh area near the beach.

But, thankfully, he not only had survived but had bought a kholi (one room accommodation) each for four of his brothers in Bombay, which were worth five million rupees now—he said. He made Govinda think of the movies churned out by the film industry of Bombay, based on similar themes: where the paupers from the villages come to the city and make it big. A theme so epitomized by the films of the Bollywood superstar Amitabh Bachchan.

The passenger also told Govinda that the legal case he was fighting was a dispute about the land and only his grandson could expect to have a verdict on it. The lawyer will bleed him financially--he was worried.

(Three)

It was in the summer of 1987, that Govinda first came to the railway station of Gorakhpur, on his way to Ahmedabad: an industrial city in Gujrat province of India. He was going there for an interview for a job in a reputed corporate house. Not aware of the regulations of the railways, he was found without a ticket on the platform and paid the fine.

Unlike the last time however, he was aware this time that deaths were being reported due to dengue fever, Japanese Encephalitis and malaria almost every day by the newspapers, from the area he will be traveling through, and he will have to be very careful to avoid a mosquito bite therefore; apart from avoiding catching water-born diseases.

He had heard of youngmen dying of encephalitis in a Kathmandu hospital, after they returned from a tour of the affected area; and met a young woman who caught elephant-feet after a similar trip, and walking unsteadily ever after, when one of her legs grew monstrously big. Until this day, when she has grown old to become a grandmother, she complains why she ever visited that plain area in summer.

Once his father told him a few years before his death that he was glad to have survived the seventy-eight years of his life. He said that there are various situations in life one passes through, and it was a long time to have survived all those years. Many of the people he had seen dying young. Some of them died in an accident and others due to different diseases they caught due to an unhealthy lifestyle.

Govinda had similar thoughts in his mind standing on the railway station of Gorakhpur, on that afternoon, while the train was waiting to leave on a two-day long journey. He purchased a religious book of Gita Press Publication of Gorakhpur, glad to find its stall at the same place on the railway platform, as he did when he came here the last time. That time too he had purchased another religious book.

Some of the books of Gita Press and its regular Kalyan monthly magazine made a part of his readings in his childhood, as other books were rare where he grew up, apart from the textbooks.

The descriptions of the religious stories did not engage him much in Kalyan Magazine, as he grew up. But he read them in those times nonetheless, as they were there, in those issues of Kalyan; which were reverently handled by even the people who could not read. It was impossible to reject something which so many people believe in, for him.

With the book of Gita Press in his hand, his mind drifted to the various thoughts occurring to him one after another. Surviving those years since his last visit to Gorakhpur away from his home appeared to him like a lifetime by itself. He had to support himself on every count and had to bear many family responsibilities, like financing the education of his brother or the medical treatment of his father.

In spite of his youthfulness and a good health, which he had built in his days in the college, hoping to become a professional athlete, the hope he abandoned realizing that a taller good athlete will always beat a smaller good one like him; there were times of sickness and the consequent physical or emotional frailties.

Returning to his parents was not a choice, as there was no promise of a future there. The responsibilities increased as he decided to marry a woman of his own choice, rejecting the ones his father had found for him. Moreover, they had children over the years. The schooling of the children had started when they grew up, and they were now going to colleges. He lingered on in the same job, as he had decided to give up the hopes of having a career, as there were very few around that were genuine.

He thought he would just make a living. This situation made him arrange his life with the small amount of salary he earned. However, he kept the needs of his family limited. Something always restrained him for going for jobs that promised better money but were tyrannical in nature, or entailed a lot of manipulating skills. For him being at peace to focus on his hobbies was more important.

He found himself saying goodbye to most of his friends, who were joining the mainstream, hoping to have a career in it. A few of them became alcoholic and died very young and some others turned paupers, as their ambitious business venture failed. But there were some success stories too, where a friend establishes an industry and became rich.

He knew that most of the people scoffed at his ideas about life. But he preferred it this way: A life less crowded by the people who had different interest. He had promised himself that he would never go for making best of the worst—as it appeared to him. So, on one hand the world was shrinking for him, on another it was expanding.

Anything which threatened to alter his equilibrium, which he thought he had achieved after building a life that he chose, he avoided. Nevertheless, at times, it appeared if he was losing the sight of the way ahead. On his completion of forty years, a friend of his wife wished that he might live another forty years. It was also the birthday of Goninda's wife too as per the lunar calendar on that day. They had invited her to celebrate it. The first thought that occurred to him on hearing it was: "for what?"

Govinda thought, earlier, that he recognized the UP state roadways bus driver who had driven it to Gorakhpur from the Nepalese border town called Sunauli. He appeared to Govinda to be the same person, who did so the last time he was here. Only that he had lost most of his teeth on the front and had all white hair on his head. For he drove it slowly, took frequent breaks and argued with the passengers who complained about it.

The bus was as dilapidated as he remembered, and climbed with a great difficulty a small height, at one place it came across, after the driver frantically shifted the gears-- though it was only half full of passengers.

Govinda thought if he was mistaken or was too romantic, to have a thought like that--that he recognized a driver who drove the bus for four hours, in which he happened to be there, so long back.

The bus conductor did not return the change and instead wrote it on the back of his ticket, asking Govinda to collect it later from him, as he did not have the change. Govinda recalled that he forgot to recover the money many times on the UP state roadways buses on previous occasions, similarly written on the back of a ticket. He made sure that he did recover it this time, before he reached Gorakhpur, by himself arranging change from a fellow passenger.

He had become clever enough to know that once you reach a destination you become mentally engaged about the next--to forget about your money due on a bus-conductor.

....

There were two elderly women pilgrims with him, on his bus from Kathmandu to Sunauli. They were from Bombay and were returning after visiting Mansarover Lake which is situated in Tibet and is a very important destination for Hindu pilgrims, as mountain Kailash, the mythological abode of lord Shiva, is situated near that lake.

It was difficult to imagine that they have undertaken the journey at their age and on their own, as they were only housewives. They informed Govinda that visiting Mansarovar is easier from Kathmandu--while they complained about how so many people are out there to cheat or short-change the pilgrims like them. They also complained that none of the governments of both the countries had made any special arrangements for the people like them.

They checked the price of everything that the vendors brought into the bus, before saying that it was cheaper in Tibet, as most of the goods the vendors were selling were Chinese. They did not purchase anything--not even the corn on the cob, which one of them tasted after picking a grain from it and then said that it was not hot enough so tasted stale. The woman Nepalese vendor made a face on it, while the fellow passengers smiled.

(Four)

One was told that the rain-gods were kind this time and most of the dams in central India were over-flowing. It was the reason that one did not come across the newspaper stories of the ceremonies of the marriages of frogs, ritually under taken by people in an area receiving no rains in the monsoon season, or of the women of a village dancing naked in the daylight in the open, to attract the rain gods, after locking all men of the village in their homes.

Last year a yagna was undertaken by the people in another area, where the crops started to die in the absence of the rains. In a yagna large quantities of grains and milk-fat are burnt, to appease the rain gods. In the absence of any rain-water harvesting idea at the common level, the people continue with their traditional ways to cause rains.

So there will be a good harvest ahead, for this year at least, before people again begin looking skywards for the rains the next summer. It was good news from an area that was mostly in news for social distress lately, apart from the suicides of farmers.

....

Next morning, on resuming the conversation, Rakesh informed Govinda that the things were fine now, as the oncologist has informed him after the recent quarterly follow-up. He could also be grafted with artificial teeth now, on his right, lower grafted jawbone. He told his goal now was mustering money for that operation. He added that the Tata cancer hospital in Bombay was his new place of pilgrimage now, where he will have to periodically reach for the follow-up.

....

Now back in his apartment in Kathmandu, thinking about the harrowing tale of Rakesh, an electronic engineer who was happy to be a clerk in a government department, who was an innocent victim of an ignorant and indifferent culture, Govinda felt shaken.

He could feel the tranquilizer tablet taking its effect. He reclined on his bed and closed his eyes. He hoped to be in a better mood in the evening--while chewing the nicotine gum.

The chain of endless thoughts has completed a sentence in his mind.
He was happy about that.

City-Women and the Ghost-Writer

A friend of mine has been rendered out of job at present, as the people in power — whose auto-biographies he wrote earlier, after interviewing them and making notes over the months — have suddenly run out of resources, due to the unstable political situation of the country.

Even the private publishers shy away from publishing such books nowadays, as, like before, their sale to even the state-owned libraries too is not assured. It is difficult now to predict if a person will remain in an office of power six months or a year down the line. The publishing company owned by the government, which published most of such autobiographies earlier, edited by someone politically appointed, has no space to store such ghost-written autobiographies and has to dispose those volumes as scrap. The funds allocated for this industry have become scarcer too, due to increasing scrutiny of the public. So the ghost writers have fewer customers now.

My friend began his writing career by self-publishing short satirical poems as a very thin book, of a poor quality paper. He sold it by reading/singing from it — loudly — after he took a copy from a bag containing more books, making his way in the crowd, in a local bus waiting for more passengers.

He proudly proclaims nowadays, whilst telling the story of his struggle for survival in the city, that his inspiration was a newspaper hawker, who worked earlier as a helper boy in a city-bus, when he was a child. He became a journalist and newspaper publisher later, and nowadays he owns a palatial building and many flashy cars. Such rags to riches stories, he mentioned, inspired him, that also entailed flirting with an intellectual occupation like journalism or poetry-writing.

My friend later also tried his luck with a few other genres, including fiction-writing. He personally met the people — whose auto-biographies he had ghost-written earlier — to present them with a copy of his book, when there were no more auto-biographies for him to write. He hoped that they would arrange the purchase of his book by the government libraries, in which these people were trustees or they had connections.

It did not work, however. His book sold only a few copies. In one instance he found a copy of it he had signed to a former-minister kept for sale, second-hand, on a footpath-shop. That shop also sold used foreign magazines with big pictures of half-naked women. Most of the material on sale there was separated from the scrap.

My friend later wrote a letter to the editor of a newspaper about this issue, lamenting how disheartened he felt on finding that his personally signed book to a former-minister – who blamed his Oxford education for pronouncing Nepal as 'Nepol' – had been sold as scrap. He got many thanks from the readers for sharing his experience publicly in the following days in the Readers' Column of the newspaper. A few of the readers, curiously, had a similar story to tell.

My friend, who nowadays describes himself as a former-ghost-writer had already made his hay while the sun shone for him. He managed the migration of both of his sons to the West which is considered the final proof of one's success here. He could afford his present joblessness without a problem hence.

The idleness at times rendered him cantankerous and unreasonable, however. More so, when one of his sons lost his job in the USA, due to the present economical recession recently or due to some other reasons earlier; and he had to send him money to survive the temporary joblessness.

Sending him money was urgent else he was threatening to come back along with his green-card-holding wife of Nepalese origin, who too had lost her job—he informed. My friend's wish to have a cool retired life in the USA with his children had not materialized so far.

He no more cites the migration of his children and their establishing a life in the USA as the success story of the democracy here—as he did earlier, for to sustain it he was still sending them money.

He cleverly though had arranged the marriages of both of his sons to the green-card-holder women of the Nepalese origin.

At times, however, he complains of feeling lonely and, when there is a burglary or other crimes in his neighborhood, of insecurity. But there was a consolation for him that the parents-in-law of his sons too lived in similar circumstances in Kathmandu, apart from the many other people of his age, in his neighborhood, who too had their children migrated to the West. They all met each other often and shared news and comforted each other if it was a bad one.

One of his complains was about the wisdom of the newspaper columnists here, who speculated about the worsening recession in the USA, though the Nepalese currency had lost ten percent value against it, with in a few recent months. The US dollar had gained ten times the value against the Nepalese currency in the last two decades. At this rate he feared that Nepalese currency could become almost valueless some day against the dollar. It pinched him harder when he had to put of ever more rupees to buy a dollar when he had to send it to his sons.

'It was the power of the Western media,' I tried to reassure him, 'that the people took the US's problem more seriously than their own.'

To indulge himself however, in order to rid the boredom, he became a disciple of a cult of a late Indian guru who promoted emancipation through sex and meditation.

He took many days' resident meditation sessions in the asharam of the cult, which was situated in side a dense forest a few hours' drive away from Kathmandu. It ran those sessions many times a year which were attended by an ever growing crowd of its followers.

Those sessions were also attended by young and old lady disciples called 'main' or mother. They too were similarly seeking emancipation through the method of the late Guru.

An octogenarian, bachelor ex-Prime Minister of

Nepal had been also frequenting the asharam recently, on a wheelchair, helped by his many lady attendants. The ex-PM had a scandalous reputation about his sex-life, in a society where getting married is almost a norm.

My friend returned everytime happier from those sessions and smiled for many days afterwards, without an apparent reason. Soon, his second wife, who lived with him in Kathmandu and was many years younger to him, became suspicious and discovered the dubious reputation of the cult. My friend had to stop visiting that ashram, afterwards.

His resentment of the people writing in English remained, as they were found to be mysteriously maintaining a lavish lifestyle, though there was never much audience for English writing at home. As I suspected, he also had a poor understanding of it.

He thought that the people with English language skills here were only good at conning others —incapable of doing a worthwhile job. No wonder, the illiterate people, making the majority, though admiring the native people with the English education, always looked suspicious, if they actually had to deal with them.

He compared my writing in English to Hindi-speaking of the migrant Nepalese workers, in the town where he lived most of his student-life, in the Northern India. Their earnest emphasis on vowels, while trying to speak in Hindi, left the native-speakers choking with laughter. He doubted if my English writing elicited a similar response, among the native speakers abroad — if anyone cared to read my work.

He had lived in Kathmandu most of his working life hobnobbing with the high and mighty — who could afford his ghost auto-biography-writing of their's.

Those autobiographies attracted a few incredulous readers, but caused a few secretly solicited and duly rewarded 'book-analysis', in the newspapers, by yet another breed of the writers and columnists; who took time-off from writing the dubious but sponsored project reports of different non Govrnmental Organisations, where they did their regular jobs. Those books were mostly purchased by the library the government owned.

His unchanged rustic manners irritated me. It was a comfort that he was a person of limited and predictable intellectual means, and hence not a real threat, therefore. In spite of his ridicule of my work, our friendship survived therefore.

The refinement of the urban women amazed him greatly, and he could never be sure about the age of an urban woman he met. He said it was because of their being dressed and made-up so well. He lamented the disadvantage of the village women who worked hard all their lives and had no means to amuse or make-up themselves with.

They became almost invariably old after bearing and rearing--often more than two--children, soon after they got married--at an earlier age than the city women. City women had fewer children and spaced their pregnancies successfully.

When I said that there were some women in the villages much better-off and with no real work, he pointed to the lack of objects to amuse themselves with, in a village. I could not demure much beyond that point.

His skepticism had not deterred him from marrying a young city woman as his second wife, in his late middle-age, and abandoning his first wife and his only daughter living at his village.

It was for many years that he had not visited them. But he regularly sent money to them, to take care of their limited needs beyond the things that were produced in the village.

Which were commodities like the industrial products of daily need, such as detergents, clothes, tea-leaves; and sugar etc.

He was surprised that during his childhood days very few people drank tea in his village, and raised crop of sugarcane to make their own sugar – though as a big spherical yellow-brown blocks of Gur, and not the white grains of industrial refined sugar.

But now every household in the villages too needed tea two times a day, like in the city. He blamed it on the people retired from the British-Indian military, who brought the tea-leaves home during their holidays, and spread the habit among the villagers.

I was thankful that he did not denounce this habit as feudalistic, as was his wont—whenever he spoke about the disparity in the society and the disadvantaged groups. Their cause he seemed to champion mostly, in the casual talks.

The people who could not offer tea to a visitor were considered really poor in a village. People offered milk-tea to their guests they wanted to genuinely welcome and black-tea to the others who were less than welcome.

Drinking milk or its products by a not-so-welcome guest was feared to invoke a bad omen, to negatively affect the supply of milk from the livestock, or cause other serious misfortunes to the host.

However, this newly-acquired social necessity of offering tea to a guest had created a kind of divide among the otherwise self-sufficient and equal villagers, as per my friend.

My friend was not aware that his second, unbefitting marriage, due to the age disparity, was a matter of ridicule among the people, who knew him. It was more of an envy, as having marital relations among the city-dwellers was considered a kind of achievement for the villagers, who had migrated to the city out of poverty mostly, and managed to sustain themselves in the hostile circumstances in it.

They were resented in their villages for their betrayal for not marrying a woman from their society, or for deserting her – as was the case with my friend. During his tough days of struggle he felt very lonely and without an emotional support in a hostile city. Then he fell in love with the daughter of the landlord of the house where he lived in a rented room and they got married.

He tried to keep contact with his first wife but was rebuffed. Then their daughter's marriage was arranged after many years in which he spent a good amount of money to appease his first wife. On it she relented a little but had never forgiven him completely.

....

The considerations of caste or community had to be set aside in such marriages between a villager and a city-woman. If one got trapped in a marriage with a lower-caste woman of the city – or in a contrary situation for a woman – then there was no escape from it often.

Marriage continues to apply a kind of finality in the lives of the people, of a certain type, even in the city. Else why would the people have the air of a sacrificial glory about them on their marriage-day? Marriage is a type of gamble that makes or breaks the people in their later lives, in various ways.

Some people take it as a political move and wait, putting their instincts on hold, for the best match that could enhance their career prospects. The tyranny of the hierarchy of caste or community is no less rigorous in the city, as it is in villages. It is around the institution of marriage that they are observed the most. No wonder the people marrying outside their caste or community become communists, in many cases.

Keeping a mistress was something a few people could afford here, though it often is the next in hierarchy of needs, next to the fulfillment of basic needs and before the self-actualization. It is an expression of the sign of security which comes with affluence mostly.

Also, the women, who are willing to remain a mistress for life, are in short supply, in spite of widespread poverty, though not totally absent. The government often provided some amount of money in a fixed deposit maturing at a later date, for the dowry of a girl, who became orphaned in a natural or man-made disaster, thereby furthering the institution of marriage.

The people, therefore, who could afford to marry twice or more often, did so--wearing the air of sacrificial glory about them every time, without having any serious problem from their first wife if they financially maintained them — like my friend did.

A second wife of a man could be a willing woman of a much younger age, from a family with financial problems and with too many daughters to marry. Even though there are laws against polygamy, polyandry too remains prevalent in certain hilly-parts of the country.

Recently, an ex-minister of the now ousted Royal Government and a former army helicopter pilot died at the age of around fifty. He had earlier resigned from his army job to own a company running many helicopters on hire. It was reported that he got multiple kidney-transplants in India, donated by some among his five wives. This is how the matters are irrespective of what is written in the law-books. The ex-minister did not survive as his body rejected the transplanted kidney every time.

....

Sending children abroad was the next step in climbing higher in the hierarchy of the society. Now there are reports that such migrants did extremely menial and low-category jobs in the Europe or the USA, which they would have felt embarrassed to do here — and had made a fortune here too, if they had worked as hard in those kinds of jobs.

Very few of the migrants could return with the university degrees, which they claimed they were trying to earn in those countries — on their holidays here. Some of those, who did earn their degrees abroad, remained unemployed here, after they returned and tried to make a living — not finding any use of the knowledge they had acquired, except for working in a job that needs them to continuously seek outside money, to improve the lives of the majority of this country.

A relation returned with a post-graduate degree in Philosophy from the USA, and opened a counseling centre in the heart of the Kathmandu city, after his interview was published in a local vernacular weekly, owned and edited by another relation, presenting him as a success-story, for getting a proper education in the USA.

He expected the people to come to him for an advice, for a fee. No one came, and people instead speculated about the business he had started — so unheard of until then. Soon he got the correct advice himself from another relative: that the people here advise each other so freely that no one may come to him for it, after paying a fee. The wise man took the advice and closed-down his counseling centre, and returned to the USA, for further studies — one was told.

I asked a British lady, who had worked as a psychotherapist all her life in Britain: why she thinks that fewer people are practicing her specialty here. She frankly told me that the psychological problems could only be noticed and treated if one had enough food on the table. I could not agree more.

It may be the reason that the youngsters are groomed — by the system of education and their family — mostly to become either a doctor or a lawyer--the disciplines which earn one a fortune in a diseased and illiterate society. They are the professionals consulted most by the people after paying a fee here.

However, the privileged ones — those who have manipulated the anomalies of their society to become privileged themselves, and made things worse for the rest — have little faith here, on the competence of the health professionals, and go away to the USA or Europe, to get treated for even the minor diseases. Some of the wealthy and influential people, speculatively, died here, due to wrong diagnosis — those who tried to put faith in the system of healthcare here.

There are reports of stolen kidneys of the people who admitted themselves for ENT surgeries, at a private hospital, suggesting if the modern education has helped mostly to cheat better here, as my friend often doubted.

An eminent neurosurgeon and an ex-Health Minister of the Royal Government, formed after the last coup by the King, once, while in office, alleged that most of the gynecologists drive around in their four-wheelers they bought from the money they made by performing — then illegal — abortions.

A few practicing gynecologists contested his claim. One suspected that the gynecologists earlier lobbied to keep the abortion illegal till many years after the democracy ushered— in, in the country, to perform it secretly at their private clinics, at a high fee. After the abortion was legalized here, a few years ago, this industry has suffered a set—back. Even the public hospitals some senior doctors used to tun as their fief earlier. In one case an ear surery reportedly took place in the eye hospital at Tripureshwar, as the surgeon performing it was a friend of the director of the hospital and a private practioner.

There could be taken — however — a consolation from the news that, the people, who went abroad to get themselves treated, found at least one native doctor in the team that treated them. One can not help but take pride in the things a few people from here, are doing so well, abroad.

For those, so many in numbers, who achieve no such merits there, and do small—time jobs, who mostly return, after their visa could not be extended further, with small fortunes out of their years of hard labour, lamenting the discrimination they suffered for being an outsider in those countries.

They had earned just enough though, to buy a house and a car in the capital. They could be noticed with their cars often in the queue at a gas station, due to the infrequent supply of the petroleum.

They drive around mostly to meet their relations, to show—off themselves and their families, or for receiving or giving advices. At times they also may be seen patronizing the expensive restaurants, frequented by tourists otherwise.

Migrating for making a living is undoubtedly becoming popular here, as even the government's postal department has started filling—in and electronically submitting the US diversity visa lottery, for a fee — putting up a stiff competition for the private cyber—café owners of Kathmandu, or in other smaller towns in the country.

It resulted in bringing down remarkably the cost of the service over the years. In this instance the government of Nepal was found stealing the private jobs instead of creating the same: the type of jobs which are created out of the joblessness of the people, in the first place.

After all it continues to be advised by a large number of consultants employed by the donor community, who rarely know the problems of the people, though they are equipped with many sets of solutions.

This situation has prevailed here in spite of the frequent political revolutions, even when the last one has established a 'New-Nepal', ousting the King. Fewer of the governments around, however, could claim not to be stealing from the people, in one way or another.

My friend's had been a life of genuine survival during a time when only limited intellectual curiosities and indulgences were tolerated and rewarded. His habit of changing a topic, if the discussions turned serious, was in fact a technique he had acquired over the years, in his professional life of a ghost-writer. So he was mostly not a bad company.

His curiosity to observe the things around, which were so different than his peasant life in the village where he grew up; and the small Indian town, where he went for schooling, has remained intact.

His pretensions at writing made him come out more eloquently--orally, on the things he noticed, in his native, rustic language. Sometimes his observations and commentaries were really remarkable. Though they also, ironically, betrayed his peasant background and the limited insights he had about life.

....

On the other day, he discussed about a middle-aged city woman, who was coming to his house to do the laundry once a week, for the last few years. She was short but was sturdily built. She had fair skin and sharp features.

Her arms looked powerful and tight skin on her face suggested a good health. But some sadness too was noticeable on it, accentuated by the wrinkles next to her eyes.

He said she arrived so well-dressed and made-up on her high-heeled sandals that it was difficult to differentiate her from the Gharania (upper-class) women of the city.

As soon she arrived she changed into a worn out nightie, which had to be slipped on from the head, which she produced from her cheap but trendy bag hanging from her shoulder.

Then she sat for the rest of the day on the heap of clothes to be washed in the front-yard of his house enjoying the winter-sun simultaneously. A pipe continuously supplied water from a backyard tank to the many plastic buckets in bright colours; and a wide-rimmed metal container. She first applied soap to the laundry and then risnsed by twisting and manipulating it while soaked in clean water. Then she emptied the containers of used-water. The heaps of laundry continuously shifted from one container to another.

My friend complained that she used too much of water. The thousand-liter water-tank in his backyard got emptied every time she washed at his home. He had to worry about filling it for the next time, from the irregular water-supply of the city, with the help of a manual pump – an exercise which kept his servant busy for a few mornings, and away from the other chores.

He said he could not afford to buy clean water in a tanker, like many of his neighbours--which he got earlier for free, when his brother was working in the Department of Water Supply of the government, before he got transferred out of the city.

By evening she filled the drying ropes arranged in the compound with dripping clothes for drying. It took a few days for the laundry to dry, after it was spread one-by-one in the sun of the winter which was feeble on most days due to mist in Kathmandu.

Besides it was obstructed by the growth of a guava

and a pomegranate tree in his compound as sun prenetrated at a slanting angle during winter for only a few hours a day. In summer she washed in the backyard of the house and the laundry dried in a day.

Then she was offered by his wife an enormous meal of chyura (beaten-rice), a day or older meat-dish and freshly cooked vegetables and pickle. Tea followed in the last after she had finished her meal. His wife spoke to her in their common Newari mother tounge in a friendly manner and he could not understand a word of it.

Afterwards she changed back in the fashionable dress in which she had arrived, and put on the make-up, peeping into a mirror she produced from her bag.

Neatly she packed the worn-out nightie into it, along with the other things. She left with a five-hundred-rupees note as a payment and the soap and detergent she had saved from the washing, to use it at her home. On her high heels which made a sound at her every step on the concrete floor of his compound she looked no-less presentable than any other, upper-class city-woman.

Whenever she asked about increasing her wages she was offered an additional cake of soap, but seldom the money by his wife.

Her washing was good and high in demand. I realized it when my offer, through my friend, to wash similarly at my home was declined by her with the regret that she was booked for almost every day of the week and had almost no time even for her family.

During the day her children remained at school on most days of the week, but there were holidays too, at times, when she had to be with them. She had no time for it.

I also realized that she was earning more than most city women who worked in the offices, government or others, who went around on an Indian or Chinese made two-wheeler, bought on hire-purchase mostly, in the streets of Kathmandu, though her job was not easy.

My friend further informed me that she had been working to raise and educate her two daughters, finding that her alcoholic husband was not showing any signs of improvement. She was a house wife earlier when her husband had a job in an insurance company. But he became an alcoholic due to the bad company of friends he found there and lost his job. Then she started to work. She not only paid all the bills of the family but also gave limited money to her husband to buy alcohol every day.

I could not help but admire this, yet another, city-woman, who had accepted a life of hard work to raise and educate her children, but was discreet enough to maintain her presentable appearance. This type of cleverness is difficult to find among the village-women, my friend complained, in his usual way. I agreed readily.

The Spiritual Escape

He boasted of belonging to a renowned family of the past, and also a relation with the owner of the company, in which he had been, though, working in a junior position for many years now. His small pot-bellied body suggested that he had never been used to physical labour of any kind. His name was Ramesh.

Recently, while a colleague was collecting donations to renovate a dilapidated but ancient temple on the outskirts of Kathmandu in his village, I too contributed whatever I could. Ramesh had a habit of contributing more than his capacity in such social causes. His spendthrift wife flied away every alternate month to see her parents. Two able-bodied but indolent brothers-in-law in their late twenties have been staying with them now for the past several years. They ostensibly were looking for a job in the city; preferably a civilian type, as they feared the rigours of an army or a police job — the two types mostly on offer here, which also needed very little academic qualifications to join.

Police or army jobs also were riskier now due to the escalating Maoist insurgency. Ramesh always ran short of money maintaining his family. Obviously, he alone could not afford so many expenses, with his paltry-paying job.

On that day he opened his wallet in front of everybody only to find that it was empty except for a small change. He asked me, saying that since he forgot to keep any money in his wallet in the morning, that if I could lend him five-hundred rupees. He said he would pay me back the next day. Since I had the money, I gave it to him.

He contributed two hundred rupees to the temple renovation fund — twice than I had, and kept the change with him. He said to my inquiring countenance that going around with empty wallet was not proper for him as you do not know when you might need some cash during the day.

He repeated that he would return my money the very next day. For a month I kept my patience, while I did not receive any, before I inquired about my money, not – out of hesitation – with Ramesh, but with the some other colleagues, who were present when I lent Ramesh the sum.

A colleague, barely able to hide his smile, told that everyone except me in the office knew that Ramesh was a bad debt re-payer, and owed some money to almost everyone in the office including the peon.

The colleague also told me that Ramesh complains of forgetfulness nowadays on account of a thyroid disease he said he is suffering from. This claim he substantiated readily with a prescription he produced from his shirt pocket – particularly when he is reminded of a loan-repayment date by a colleague.

Also, Ramesh never forgot those who denied him a loan on asking, and discussed it with other colleagues lamenting the meanness of them. After all, who does not run into financial problems once in a while, he said, to justify his loan-taking and repayment-forgetting position.

Clearly he was suffering from a – real or fake – profitable disease and when I hesitantly asked him to pay back my loan a few days later he said he had no recollection of taking any loan from me.

Now, being aware of his problem, I decided to forget my money. Thinking that at least the God in the heaven knows who actually paid for the renovation of one of his dilapidated temples, in the outskirts of the Kathmandu city. I felt frustrated and angered at the same time for my inability to recover my money from a soft-spoken and well-mannered person like Ramesh, who criticised his wife and in-laws only to win sympathy and cash as a loan from a friend.

That evening I decided to go for a walk to a Buddhist monastery on top of a hillock near my apartment, as I felt bugged by so many day-to-day issues of the similar nature. They were trivial to discuss with others but financially exacted a cost. Discussing such matters with my wife I had abandoned a long time ago, as she rebuked me, instead of showing any empathy.

I have found over the years that such visits to religious places gave me the spiritual-dexterity to handle the cumulative emotional-burden of such situations and helped restore my calm and poise to carry on with life.

At the bottom of the steep, countless steps leading to the monastery, I saw a drunken middle-aged man slapping his wife. She was trying to attend a customer simultaneously, while arguing with her husband; who was asking her for some money for buying liquor; on her pushing-cart selling vegetables. Soon their teenage son came to the rescue of his mother and chased away his father with some arguments and stern warnings.

The whole scene was not conducive for the spirituality I wanted to seek by climbing those uphill-steps to reach the monastery. I chose to forget about what I had witnessed and climbed up.

The view from the monastery of the Himalayas in the north was as relaxing and reassuring as ever. Those proud white-mountains always promised a continuity and stability amongst the everyday chaos and confusion. Aero planes could be seen taking off or landing, at the airport in the east. Some of them just came over the monastery soon after the take off and then tured in different directions.

Oh it is a Fokker--I thought, as the engines were attached on the tapering rear of the plane, instead of on the wings. I had learnt to recognize some of the planes flying by their shape, and the airlines of different countries by their logos.

In the beginning with the help of an article published in an on-board magazine of the then Royal Nepal Airlines, with the drawings of different aero planes and the logos of different airlines, I practiced recognizing them when they were flying from the roof of my apartment. In a short time I could recognize most of the aircrafts flying here.

During night I similarly saw them landing or taking-off, from my apartment-roof, but not recognizing any. Appearing first as a dot of light in the night sky

like a star, it was coming near and becoming bigger by the seconds. Turning into multiple lights, as it came closer, it turned to the left or right, to approach the airport, to land. Watching aircrafts fascinated me always.
....

The rest of the landscape was occupied by modern buildings made of concrete and red-bricks, topped by the hoarding-boards filled with colourful advertisements or antennae of different shape and size.

The crowded dwellings of the people in the city appeared like a trap which was difficult to break. Hardly any space was visible between the houses, just like in an all consuming relationship.

The hills were there surrounding the Kathmandu valley on all the sides. They promised a lot of green forests and possibly unaltered natural landscapes beyond them — quite contrary to what was visible.

I thought one could nearly miss the larger picture, around the city or life, if one did not care once in a while to look at things from somewhere higher.

The constructions, designs and the crowd around obstruct the vision so totally that one might never be able to see beyond the immediate. In a way the world one sees is only a limited vision from a perspective, and things could start to look very different, if looked at from another. The occupations of life have somehow made those areas remote for me, from where I could look at things afresh--I thought. I wondered if I will have the time and resources ever to go there and feel good for just being there out of the trap, from where I could look at things more differently and clearly.

These thoughts, though transient like most, and a product of melancholy and regret, calmed my nerves, and I thought about visiting a few nearby Hindu-temples too, to make my spiritual-escape of that evening a little more perfect.

I went down the stairs of the monastery to find that the woman was still smiling and doing a brisk-business on her vegetable-selling cart. Her husband and son were not in sight. I, nearly meditating, walked past the small bazaar on my way to the Krishna Temple and Durbar square of Patan, a little high on the dose of spirituality I have imbibed – I thought – through the contemplation, so recently.

The sight of the black-coloured Krishna temple, which was made of carved stones and nothing else, and had been an object of belief for so many people over more than two centuries now, filled me with a soothing piety and humility, when I reached there.

The three-storied pyramidal temple, placed nearly two-meters higher than the ground, has windows which give a pleasing view of the Durbar Square of Patan. But one has to enter it through the narrow, low metal-doors and then climb equally narrow steps of the poorly lit small stairs, risking a fall always, due to the continuous traffic of the people going up or down; while continuously minding one's head, due to a very low roof, to reach those windows. Besides the temple opens only for a short time late every evening for prayers only, so there is no time to enjoy the view out of those windows.

It also opens for public for a whole day on the birthday of lord Krishna. But it is very crowded on that day, when the King too visits this temple in the evening.

Devotees have to make a rush to see and be seen there on that day. The boys, who look after the shoes that one has to leave behind before entering the temple, charge a small fee for their service. Unattended--the shoes are certain to disappear.

There remains a sense of hustling and hoarding in the air near the Krishna temples of Patan on that special day, like in other major Hindu temples, instead of the calm and tranquility one expected. Devotees are extorted of money for goods or services which are often not necessary and are made scarce by hoarding, after cramming them in a limited space. No wonder there have been stampedes in such gatherings and many people have lost their lives or have been permanently disabled.

My heart however, went to the people, who took the pain to erect the Krishna temple – so heavenly and inspiring even today.

The short winter day was about to be over and the darkness was slowly enveloping the sky. But I lingered-on around the Krishna temple, lost in my thoughts, relishing the sight of it. It was rapidly becoming nearly invisible in half-darkness, due to its black color.

Soon the lights were switched-on and whole of the Durbar square became flooded by it. In that dazzling light the Krishna temple looked more mysterious then before. It was shining due to the humidity it had collected as if it was painted freshly. It was time to go for me.

In my heart, before I left, I made a promise that I would return as soon as I could, to pay homage to Lord Krishna and the people who built the monument there. The remorse in my heart, against Ramesh or other people was no more there now, and I genuinely felt happy for a moment.

The very thought that there are so many things around, which I do not understand but have to pay the respect to, for their inexplicability, was humbling, as well as unsettling. Life has always been routed by such opposite notions, as it may seem to one.

While returning home, I recalled that, I had to buy vests for my younger son, whose size wasn't easily available often. I went to a well-lit shop in the Durbar-square itself.

The Malla King of Patan resided here long back and had made spaces for his indulgences like many other small temples and open lobbies besides the Krishna Temple in that area. The water sprout behind his palace must have had bathing women during the day, on them he must have ogled at from the behind the carved windows which had wooden net on them.

Those spaces in the Durbar square now served as shops though they were no less archaeologically important than the Palace of the King, now serving as a museum—across the road.

In the shop I found a fair and overweight shopkeeper, who was balding and smiling.

His manners were slow and meditating. I thought it

could be because his shop was so near to the Krishna Temple of Patan. For a moment I thought if I could fathom the depth of his spiritual-calmness, extrapolating it with the effect the short visit of mine had on me to this temple.

Not visiting a nearby temple for too long left me feeling guilty, as everyone else seemed so prompt to do this job in the society. I got lost once again somewhere within me and lost the sight of the context and the proceedings.

I just remember that I asked for two vests and paid the money and returned, taking the bag handed-over to me, after saying thanks meditatingly to a shopkeeper who looked even more meditating and more spiritually-accomplished and at peace than me.

On reaching home my calm appeared threatened once again, when my wife opened the bag and informed me that there was only one vest. When I insisted that there must be two, she handed over the bag to me.

I was not in a mood to spoil my calmness which I had achieved that evening after so many efforts. I quietly thanked the God for giving me the opportunity to visit the Krishna temple again so soon, besides the nearby, spiritually-happy shopkeeper, to recover from him the second piece of vest, for which I had paid the money.

I promised in my heart though, that, no matter how much I meditated – or the shopkeeper did – I would never forget to check the goods I purchased, in the future. It was after I recovered the vest the next evening, which became contrary of the previous meditating and happy one, as the shopkeeper and I argued and lost our cool over the matter.

....

The city bus I was returning in, later, was held-up in the traffic jam, further eroding my peace of mind. On enquiring I came to know that the jam was caused by the stopping of the motorcade of the in-office Prime Minister, who had stopped on his way to his residence, to buy a supply of *Pan* (betel leaf wrapping the betel nuts and other spices) from a shop at Kupondol.

This shop supplied him the *Pan* always whether he was a prisoner or a Prime Minister--the two roles into which some people alter here with precarious and unconvincing frequency, and a very short notice.

However, that kind of display of simplicity--which the PM perhaps wished his act of buying-pan symbolized-- by that octogenarian politician, I did not find endearing that day.

It obstructed the movement of so many people on the road. He is also a comical character due to his much-rumored sex life in spite of being a bachelor. He lives-- now in the Prime Minister's residence too--with so many of his young women-aids. His legendary talent to joke-off the serious issues of the people is often another exhibition of his simplicity.

He was also photographed this time with his feet wearing shining-shoes put on the tea table in front of the chair he was sitting on; in his national dress; soon after his oath-taking ceremony as the PM from the King.

The Delhi-return

It was a town called Munsa where brisk-business took place during the day, when the people living in the neighbouring villages came.

Most men of working age were employed either in the army or in the private companies in the distant cities, who came home on leaves regularly, as they were not paid enough to keep their families with them.

The elderly or retired former job-holders on pensions, and women and children largely populated those villages permanently, apart from the young, jobless men. The people frequently came to Munsa to sell fresh milk, fruits or vegetables they produced – to buy the things of daily need, in exchange. Some came just to hang-out, as agriculture, which was the main occupation of most of the people, employed them very sporadically.

A large number of the children from the villages came to attend the schools in Munsa daily. The town also had a bank, a hospital and a post office, which attracted more people to it. Recently, the government had contracted out the business of liquor in the town for the first time, which, sold in plastic pouches, added to the colours of the town-life. Some of the villagers drank cheap liquor almost every day from the money they mustered by selling fresh vegetables, fruits or milk, and returned home empty-handed, to their families.

The ones not able to return home, due to heavy drinking, slept on the pavements, only to return the next day. Drunken people could be seen lying unconscious in the broad daylight in Munsa streets, particularly during the days when the bank distributed pensions of the retired soldiers around the beginning of a month.

A scene earlier only appearing during a major festival of shaking drunk-men foolishly and loudly discussing the matters of a peasant life, like the cost of buying or selling of their livestock, or their conception or pregnancies, were seen everyday in Munsa.

Mainly because of the ready availability of the alcohol there more people came to the town now than before from places far away.

Previously alcohol available in the area was the only one brought home by the soldiers on-leave which they sold at a cost beyond the reach of most of the peasants.

There were increasing instances of people dying younger due to alcoholism, leaving behind young-widows and orphaned children. Wiser parents of the area hastened to send away their children, as soon they have completed the school education, to their relations doing small-time jobs in the distant cities, to get involved in some kind of job or education, but away from that – more recently – a depressing locale.

The bonhomie which prevailed in Munsa earlier, when the shopkeepers interacted with the visitors, to conduct a productive economical activity, became rarer, due to the freely available liquor--which seemed to have robbed most of the peasants of their disposable income.

The government earned a few million-rupees every year while contracting out the sale of liquor in Munsa. It was one of those ventures that sucked away the already scarce   money from the rural – like the lottery the government operated.

Lottery, which was sold through colourful tickets often depicted the image of the goddess of wealth Laxmi who has grown ever-more beautiful and slimmer in her depictions by the artists over the years, on a calendar or on a lottery ticket, while dropping gold coins from one of her many hands.

The lottery ticket seller promised through a loudspeaker held in his hand – who had many neatly arranged colourful bundles of lottery tickets in a briefcase, under a colourful umbrella, on a street-corner stall--the lottery awards in many figures. The peasants repeated those sums with disbelief or lost count of while buying the tickets.

The lottery results were published in newspapers by every month end and were avidly followed by the people. But no lottery award was ever won by someone of the locality.

The police frequently were seen taking away a troublesome drunk to their post, only to release him the next day, or the same evening, after extracting some money from that person or from the one who went to look for him.

A couple of the times the women of the area got organized and called for a strike, demanding the government to call-off the business of liquor in the town. Such movements died down without causing the desired result. All these contents made, what many thought, were a complete world, in Munsa. Out of which some got benefited, often those who were on the side of the government, like the contractor of the liquor, while others lost by becoming a victim of it.

Khurram was a peasant living in one of those nondescript villages. He had a small and a thin frame and an average height.

He too often went to the town – mostly unshaved and unwashed – in a military shirt and khaki pants, which the people, who returned on leaves to his village, had given him. During his youth he too had unsuccessfully tried his luck in the cities, to make a living. It did not work for him however, and he had to return to his village permanently instead of coming to it on leaves – like the people who on asking begrudgingly doled out to him their old and worn out clothes, shoes and blankets.

He after returning from the city worked as a tailor with his machine, scissors and chalks spread on the pavement, in front of a shop selling cloths in the town.

He made a success in tailoring, thanks to his training in the city. He later had his own shop in Munsa with a signboard which announced in bright colours:

    Khurram Tailors

    Specialists in Suits

    (Delhi-return)

The 'Delhi-return' in the last he mentioned as a qualification, in brackets, following a quack who had mentioned a few medical qualifications under his name plate in Munsa.

It spontaneously invited smiles or scorn off the people.

His shop did a brisk business for a few years. He shifted his family to Munsa in two hired rooms. He sent his children to the Private English medium school of Munsa in proper dresses.

He even renovated his ancestral house in the village where now his brother and his family lived, by plastering it on the outside and applying a very bright colour. It now looked very distinct than any other house in his village.

At the bottom of a northern hill of Munsa his village was situated in a valley on a riverbank. A road passed above it windingly climbing the hill and led to another village on top of it.

On the road there was a thin traffic of vehicles during the day. The people pasing knew which house belonged to Khurram due to its bright colour in the valley.

However, Khurram got trapped in the habit of drinking in the meanwhile. Earlier he only drank on a festival but he now needed alcohol daily.

His tailoring business started to go wrong. Soon, he sold away his shop and started to work as an assistant at a barber-shop. His family was now shifted back to his village.

He learnt some hair-cutting from his Muslim employer. Only the butcher, who slaughtered a castrated male-goat every day, except on the eleventh-day of the lunar calendar on both the sides, next to a full-moon or a no-moon day; as these two days were considered inauspicious by his all-Hindu customers to eat meat, was the only other Muslim in Munsa.

The butcher ran occasionally into trouble when he instead slaughtered a sheep or an exhausted old-goat clandestinely, not finding a castrated he-goat on a bargain, and some one divulged his mischief to his customers anonymously. Somehow he appeased his customers on this matter and his business continued in Munsa.

Due to his drinking Khurram could not stick to his job afterwards and returned to his village, which was two-hour's walk away from Munsa.

His family did a little farming there. Khurram too contributed to the domestic chores and to the work in the fields. There was little work there for his large, ever-multiplying joint family, and mostly he was idle.

The habit of drinking did not leave him, though he left the towns and the cities. Once he went on Kanystha (to look for a bride) to a neighbouring village, to marry one of his cousins who recently had got recruited in the army. He had to pass through Munsa to reach there.

In Munsa he met one of his old pals of school-days who was on leave from his army jobs and lived in the neighboring village. He was drinking in a restaurant with a bottle of rum on the table in front of him and a plate of fried fish. He asked Khurram to join him. Khurram seldom got such opportunities. He drank a copious amount of rum and ate a little fish. His friend had to leave. He gave away the remaining rum in the bottle to Khurram.

He roamed around the bazaar and slept on the pavement of Munsa between the drinks he had — for the next two days. He informed everybody, in his half-conscious, inebriated state, he met--that he was on *Kanyastha* for his cousin.

People laughed on hearing it and joked about him among them. When the daughter-in-law of the richest merchant of the town went to the temple bare-footed — carrying a covered plate with offerings she always made there on a full-moon day-- following a band of seven people in colorful uniform, many of who wore slippers instead of shoes, who played popular cinema songs to announce her journey both-ways — Khurram danced for a while, thinking if it was a marriage party — charmed by the display of grandeur in the banality of everyday in Munsa.

He was soon chased away by the bystanders. It was only after the rum got exhausted that he went on the *Kanyastha* he was talking about, in the neighboring village. In his hangover he was fooled into committing the marriage of his cousin to a cripple. But it only became apparent when the marriage ceremony has been already solemnized, and they returned home carrying the bride on a *Doli* (a wooden carriage on the shoulder of four laborers), while the groom rode an adorned horse beside it, in his regalia of a groom, including a crown of paper and plastic in bright colors on his head and a veil of golden or silver-coloured plastic threads hid his made up face.

On reaching home the bride had to descend from the *Doli* and walk into the house of the groom after kicking a pot full of rice grains at the entrance, as was the custom.

Every one saw that she walked with a limp almost half-bending her body to her left.

It was a big shock to everyone and more so for the groom, who was a tall and good-looking young man. Every one said that the marriage should be cancelled and the bride should be sent back to her home.

Then some one said that since the marriage has already taken place it could not be reversed and if he dosen't like the bride the groom was free to marry again.

After a lot of discussion the groom agreed to keep his bride. However, every one scolded Khurram for not checking the details about the bride before commiting the marriage.

So, somehow, the bride managed to kick the rice-pot with her limping leg, while standing on the good one and entered into her new home.

These days, having nothing to do at home, Khurram comes daily to the town to only look for free liquor. On certain days, when it was not available, he learnt to arrange the sale of the rum of a soldier on leave – at a premium – in the town.

In return he got some rum to drink both from the buyer and the seller. The more sales he arranged on a day, the more rum he had to drink. Though the cheap-liquor in pouches was available now in the town, the army rum was as popular as ever, for its quality.

Khurram too preferred the army-rum. On the days he

did not get any he had to satisfy himself with the cheap liquor in a pouch, which he extracted for free, from the contractor of the shop, by discussing with him his second marriage. The contractor fancied himself a romantic man, though he had a well-built, proud and domneering wife and a few children.

When Khurram discussed with him various prospective brides for his second marriage he described their figures in intimate details. The middle-aged, ugly and fat contractor shyly smiled and felt flattered on it. This ploy always yielded Khurram some liquor in a pouch.

Lately, the wife of the contractor became aware of his designs. She was angry that Khurram was promising her husband a second-marriage, in exchange for the free liquor he got. One day she called and so sternly scolded Khurram that a crowd gathered near them. Khurram went rarely to the contractor's shop afterwards and returned home without getting any alcohol to drink after passing a whole day in Munsa.

Whenever coming to Munsa, Khurram had started to keep scissors and a comb in his pocket, to work as a part-time, moving barber nowadays. He met young students on their way to the school or back and offered them hair-cutting at half the town price.

The barber of the town, who employed Khurram earlier, once called him and warned not to undercut him.

He works this way only to buy himself drinks or to meet some other pressing needs – but never to make a living – Khurram replied, to assure the barber.

On a day, when he had already had enough drinks and was returning home, a young student asked him for a haircut, the conversation was:

Student: 'Aye Khurram, can you give me a haircut?'

Khurram's fixed smile is replaced by a frown, whenever he had to concentrate. His eyes looked enraged and offended. "But I charge five rupees," he said.

"But I paid three last time."

"The time has changed now."

"I will pay you two rupees tomorrow. Give me a

hair cut now. ”

"OK. Come here and sit on this stone. ”

The young school student became a little reluctant due to the hostile conversation he was having with an elderly and drunk man.

He did not come to the place Khurram was calling him on the side of the road and awkwardly called Khurram to come to him, while trying to sit on his left ankle, while his right leg was placed in front of him.

"You want a haircut posing like a Hanuman. Come here, and make comfortable your ass on this stone, as I told you. Or I cannot give you the haircut, ” Khurram said adamently.

The student this time obeyed Khurram, a little embarrassed. He paid three rupees to Khurram after receiving the hair-cut, with no towel around his neck or the mirror in front.

After the hair cut the student paid the money instantly. Khurram kept it in his pocket with a lot of fuss – cursing people for not paying him enough whenever he did a proper job. He knew that the chances of getting the remaining two rupees were remote from that boy.

He asked the boy to dust the hairs fallen on his face and shoulder with his shirt.

Both parted ways and walked towards their villages later, as it was getting dark and cold.

The Show Goes On !

The emaciated presenter finally signed off, trying to force a smile on her mouth rendered prominent by her sunken cheeks, apparently run dry due to continuous speaking. Her spidery arms folded mechanically to make a 'namastay'.

Those arms were continuously gesticulating, equally mechanically, while she talked glibly between the commercials and the remix numbers played on the show.

The remix songs had a loud drum-sound and a matching fast rhythm of music, which was punctuated by a rigorous body-shaking of the barely clad thin models, in the visuals. The new singers sounded shallow and nasal. They disappointed profoundly to the people who had cherished the original songs. Since most of the mimicry receives the approval of the critics, and passes as creativity, complaints against it are ignored.

It was a time for news. A middle-aged, anxious looking man started to read it. He had a thin face and his hair was receding. His throat sounded bad, which he unsuccessfully tried to clear often while he read. His voice sounded like whining.

He raised his voice just as he was about to conclude reading, and tried to smile while he still talking.

When he read the score of a tennis match and the foreign names of the players and the places, nothing was clear. The confusion on his face was reinforced by the creases which often got accumulated on his forehead while he read.

The background beat given to a news story he read only made things more confusing, both for the watchers and the reader, as it became interrupted or muffled, punctuating points trivially, or stopping before one expected.

It was difficult to say if he was frowning or shrugging, after he finished reading. He looked confident only while announcing a commercial ahead. The jingle of a commercial was a relief after the gruesome details of a murder story, in which a childless old-widow was burnt alive by her neighbours, accusing her of being a witch and responsible for the death of a few young men of the village, who had drowned in the river, after the boat they were using to cross it sank due to over-load, a while ago.

On resuming he looked more miserable, and cleared his throat more frequently.

He then read news that also had a visual to his relief, as he was away from screen for a while only narrating the story.

A chief guest had to cut a ribbon to inaugurate something. The smiling chief-guest was seen sitting with the organisers, indifferent to the various announcements and querulous speeches being made in the ceremony.

Finally everybody on the stage got up for ribbon cutting ceremony. Rusty scissors were produced on an uncovered metal plate, which had bright coloured plastic rings to hold. The chief guest lifted it with one hand and with another held the ribbon, while people around him clapped in anticipation.

He smiled first to the crowd and then to the camera before he went for the cutting. The scissors were not sharp enough and did not cut.

The chief guest chose another spot on the ribbon to cut, but again failed. He smiled to the crowd again, nervously, and chose another spot. Still the scissors did not work. He looked enraged while he frantically, but unsuccessfully, tried again on several places to cut from one end of the ribbon to another.

A commotion engulfed the crowd. Finally someone from the stage cut the ribbon, after a few futile attempts, while the chief guest was touching his arm to claim symbolically, that it was actually him, who inaugurated the event. Everybody heaved a sigh of relief which could be very clearly heard, and a loud clapping followed, drowning the absurdity.

The show went on!

Sauka

The Saukas lived for three months in their homes in high mountains in summer. Rest of the time of the year they were on the move, along with their families and herds of sheep, escaping the harsh winter and doing some business in the towns of the area, in the lower, warmer lands.
Irrespective of the boundary of the countries Saukas moved with facility on either side after satisfying the custom officials--mostly with bribes--about the goods they traded in.

They passed through a town situated on the bank of a river which separated the two nations. There was another market across river in the other country. But that market was much smaller and precariously placed on big rocks making the other bank of the river.

Those rocks have survived the fierce currents of the mighty river since the time began. It was here the river passed through a very narrow passage between rocks.
From that market there could be seen the flow of the river so much down below. The white froth it churns after hitting the rocks at a great speed many times on both the sides by turns creates an awesome scene.
If anything fell from there it landed directly into the river and disappeared. The water moves in many regular perpetual circles before it moves on to a wider area where it slowes down considerably.
It left you giddy if you watched it for some time intently from a narrow lane where you were standing high above the rock the river was hitting against. The lane had shops on the other side.
Having a market there consisting of shops trading in mostly Chinese goods, varying from herbal balms and the perfumes with strange smells to the sports shoes and other such items, in the solid but small concrete buildings, created a queer scene. Some of the shops there sold alcohol prohibited on the other side of the river:

111

which was a different country. People came from locations far away from that country to have a drink in this precariously placed market above the river. The possibility of commerce decided the presence of the market in that unlikely place, and not the geography.

During monsoons every year the river gained height by a few meters and a great maltitude of its water hit those rocks with a stunning ferocity. The sound it made in doing so was angry and fearsome.

It looked as if it will crush those wrinkled rocks which always challenged its flow and the market would drop into it and disappear. It never happened however, and the water receded after the rains every time. In winter one could see the mark in the rocks many meters above the river's surface where the river flew in the peak of monsoons.

Only once did the river overflow to the extent that it entered into the market on the other side. A bridge near the narrow passage meant for pedestrians, which swung and made low, creaky sounds even if a single person walked on it, came under the level of water.

The bridge connected the two markets and the nations. It was constructed during the British Raj here. Fortunately, it was not swept away that day. Most people of the town, who had their houses near the bridge, left them to find higher ground to the north of the town.

The town until then had no electic power. People tried to assess the extent of flood with the help of feeble torches from the higher grounds, worried if it would swallow their homes and their livelihood too. That drama of nature did not cause any greater harm and the flood was gone after a few anxious hours. It receded without even touching any of the shops or houses on the other side however, which were so precariously placed on the rocks just above the river. It was because it was situated higher than the market on the side, though just above the river.

Had it flooded the shops there the people living in the rooms above them might have had to climb even higher on the steep hill behind the market.

. . . .

The Saukas often stayed there for a night or more buying and selling goods in both the markets. During this time they crossed the creaky bridge hurriedly many times. The sheep carried a bag on their backs which fell on both the sides and opened in the middle.

A grown up sheep could carry – if evenly distributed on both the sides – a total twenty kilogram weight of goods. It walked across mountains and valleys for the whole winter carrying that load, munching at the leaves it snatched from the plants on the way. The bags were off-loaded every evening from their backs.

The bags were made of a very sturdy jute material and were tightly stitched in the middle after filling evenly on both the sides, to prevent leak, theft or contamination of the goods by non-seasonal rains.

The sheep bred on the move and raised their progeny.

There were many areas in the mountains which were a few days' walk away from a market like this town, where a most essential thing like salt was available.

It was speculated that Saukas bartered their salt for grains like rice or maize – a kilogram for a kilogram. The grains then they sold in a town at a high profit to buy cheap salt again to take to another remote village on the back of their sheep.

They saved the villagers many days' walk to merely purchase salt or such other necessary things, which the otherwise self-sufficient villages could not produce. So a Sauka took the market to the villages many days' walk away, on the backs of their sheep.

The Saukas had a profound idea about the need of goods in a particular area they went to. Else they would not have been in the business they did.

Their rag-tag and often patched dresses were not indicative of their economical condition. People said that they were reasonably well-off than most. It is only to cheat the looters and thugs on the way that they camouflaged as poor in their patched clothes.

Thus they went two or three families together, along with their herds of sheep, to have a kind of moving society. It was also for security that they moved in groups. The infants were tied on the back of the parents and their grown-up children helped in controlling the herd with a stick in hand and by whistling and making querulous and forbidding sounds alternately imitating their parents. They talked in an arcane language amongst them which the children in the town tried to mockingly imitate.

They were also called *Bhotia* by the people of the area. It hinted at their Bhutani origin. But they were generally Tibetans, as they were taller than most of the hilly tribes.

Their high cheek-bones, slanting eyes and sturdily built frames testified it—apart from their strange language—that, they had nothing in common with the people of the areas they went to do business in winter.

In a group each family walked between the herds to separate one from another. It was ingenious that the sheep of different herds did not get mixed up, as their owners meticulously separated the ones that went to another herd.

I always wondered if they had secret identification marks to separate the sheep of one herd from another. None were however, apparent. How could a Sauka remember the faces of all the sheep and their lambs he owned—remained a mystery to me.

They carried the newly-born lambs on their laps until it was able to walk on its own along with the herd, while their own infants were tied on their backs, while they all moved. They released the lambs to be fed by their mothers, when they stopped to take a break or called it a day.

The sheep were of various dull colours. They all had thick curly wool covering them well. Some of them however were literally naked due to the shearing they had recently received, to yield the wool. Other gave a hint that they received the shearing sometime ago, while a few seem to call for an immediate shearing.

Saukas tied their legs and sat on top of them to harvest their wool, by grabbing it with one hand and using the scissors with the other. These people had a small stick with a top like weight at the lower end and a hook at the upper end. This equipment was continuously rotated by a Sauka by putting the stick on his thigh and then pushing it by his palm gently. It made smooth rounds of rotations for several minutes once it was set in motion.

This instrument made a yarn out of the bundle of wool, which was held in another hand of a Sauka who was operating it, stretched high above his shoulder. The yarn was collected at the lower end of the equipment above the top, after a round of rotations was over and the yarn was made to his satisfaction.

The town's children tried to make similar instruments out of a stick buried into a potato to make a yarn out of the already well-yarned cotton thread meant for stitching the cloths, or out of the cotton which was meant for dressing the wounds or making oil lamps. It was to indulge in their curiosities about a Sauka that they did so. They continued to imitate the ways and language of Saukas till the winter lasted.

The yarn of wool Saukas made in their leisure when they were on the move. Their lifestyle suggested of little leisure, however.

Their women, once they were home in the high mountains with their herd of sheep, cleverly dyed this yarn of wool to weave carpets, blankets and sweaters out of it in various attractive colours. During the months they stayed home in the summer their women sat on a frame which held many rows of threads tied at various angles into which they tied and cut the dyed yarn to make a design in a carpet or blanket.

They were to be sold during winter when they all left home to go to the towns in lower lands once again. These products were high in demand for their genuine quality.

Among the paraphernalia they carried to sustain their bohemian lifestyle were also the dried skins of the sheep they had slaughtered and eaten. The skin had its wool intact. Saukas used this skin as a mattress to sleep on during the winter. They slept in open, mostly near a river or other source of water, beside their herds. Their famous woolen blankets called *Thulma* protected them from the cold.

A *Thulma* had thick, curly sheep wool intact on the inner side and was knitted smoothly on the outer.

Their additional, on-offer *Thulmas* were readily sold in the town, as they lasted for decades and were warmer than the quilts made of cotton. Besides cotton quilts needed mending every alternate year by the people called *Dhunia*.

The *Dhunias* could be seen in the streets of a town during the beginning of a winter, with a strange instrument hanging from their shoulders. It looked as if this instrument belonged to music due to the cord it had and the sound it made. A *Dhunia* was a Muslim often and belonged to the even lower, warmer-lands, from where he came up in the hills just before the winter begun to mend or make quilts. He returned when it became colder.

While looking for a customer in the streets a *Dhunia* made that reverberating sound with the help of his instrument, to attract the attention of his customers, by pulling its cord and releasing it.

That sound became muffled when the instrument was working to mend a quilt in the hands of a *Dhunia*. Now its cord is being beaten by a wooden club, after it was placed between the dollops of cotton to be loosened.

The loosened-cotton would be put back into the sack to be stitched by a Dhunia, who always carried his big needles with him. He will then make a symmetrical design of stitches on the surface of the quilt. It was to avoid the cotton getting collected to become dollops again, while in use.

Before he stitched the quilt the *Dhunia* gave it a firm beating with a long stick to evenly distribute the cotton inside. But, somehow, the cotton inside a quilt got collected once again in dollops and it was not warm enough to protect one during winter. It needed the loosening and restiching by a *Dhunia* every few years.

A *Thulma* needed no such maintenance every few years. It was heavy and coarse to touch and needed a cotton made cover to use for some, between which it slipped continuously to get collected in the middle or in a corner due to the weight of wool it was made of. The best way to use it was by tolerating its coarseness without a cover, while enjoying the warmth it provided.

For me the Tibetan mastiff dogs of a Sauka were an added attraction. They flanked the herds – while it passed through the town – on both the sides. Those dogs were powerfully built and aggressive. It was said that they protected the sheep from predators, while their owners kept a vigil, during the nights, by burning a fire to keep away the predators.

There were stories that three or four of those dogs could take on a tiger and chase it away without a problem.

Obviously, the dogs of our town were no match for those mastiffs and retreated to a street after making a few barks of protest, while herd after herd of sheep passed through the town, separated by their owners in between, their infant tied on their backs and they carried a lamb in their bosoms and the mastiffs flanking them.

People waited and the children of the town watched in admiration while the caravan filled the small bazaar kicking the dust to create a haze that receded long after the caravan had passed away to a nearby open area on the riverbank, to make a retreat for the day.

Their owners returned to the town immediately, while their women became busy arranging dinner and doing washing on the bank of the river. They are in town now to negotiate the sale of goods they carried and to buy the things with which they loaded the sheep once again, before they moved on.

So, at times, they stayed for a couple of days near our town, offering us an opportunity to watch their lives more closely and mix with their children, who among themselves spoke a very strange language, but managed communication with us in our language. We laughed afterwards, about how they spoke our language.

Once my father explained to me that after slaughtering and consuming a sheep – which we considered unworthy of consuming, as we always preferred a castrated male-goat – they dried and carried its excess fat to cook food with later. He spat out of revulsion on such a feeding habit – as his Brahmincal instinct dictated – after he explained it to me, and said that meat products were to be consumed within a few hours after the animal is slaughtered. Also that, meat itself was an impure food and should not be eaten when it becomes stale.

But I could not share his skepticism and revulsion – though I did not demur at that time – about the feeding habit of these people called Sauka, as I was already in romance with their bohemian lifestyle, which entailed a lot of refined business skills and survival techniques. Living a secure life of a middle-class business family did not make me lose sight of the industriousness and positivism, with which these people made a living.

Today, living an even more corrupted middle-class life away from my native town, with so many unnecessary equipments near me, which try to pamper me endlessly, I hear that motorized transportation has reached those remote places. That type of herdsman have taken to a more settled type of businesses in the area – the type my family used to do – of making a living out of trading goods that others so painstakingly produce and transport.

So, rarely that type of caravan passes through that town nowadays. May be, the Saukas will pursue their new businesses with the verve I have rarely seen in the other people, instead of becoming corrupted by the settled and secured life they have opted for presently. I cannot think how they can ever give up their adventurous lifestyle for a sedentary trader's life. Let us see how it is going to transpire, however.

Parmale

Parmale was a strange character. There were stories that he had a brief married life before his wife ran away with her lover. He confirmed of his active sexual life by comparing it with eating *khir* – a dish made by rice, sugar and milk.

He was popular among the women in the neighbourhood. With them he used to talk about sexual matters in an obscene and explicit language. They crowded him in the hot afternoons of the town. The houses had the shops on the front in which their shop-keeper husbands attended the customers.

The backyard of the houses had a river next to it. The river flowed with a loud noise as it descended from high mountains, bringing in its wake a cooler wind. It made the hot evenings in the backyards of those houses, which had no space between them, a little cooler.

There the women gathered after serving the launch to their families and finishing the washing, having their evening tea while talking with Parmale.

Parmale's explicit talks left them choking with laughter, which made the dull surroundings lively and chaotic. Those women, otherwise, always appeared demure and never ventured out of their homes without the *pallu* of the sari over their head. Parmale was offered uncooked food as a reward, or a cup of tea, or some fruits – or nothing at all on some days. If provoked by those women he always came out with a joke of sexual nature.

He was equally popular among the men of the town-- who were shop keepers mostly. He tried to describe to them the figure of a woman, one of them who laughed at his jokes, gesticulating in the air with both of his hands, his face distorted due to concentration, when tempted by one of them.

He used innovative, rustic words to describe the-- slim or fat-- breasts or hips of a woman, punctuating it with his heavy but asthmatic laugh, which became nasal and broke often, as he aged.

Then he imagined aloud what it would feel like to make love to the woman he described. People gleefully listened to his innuendos for hours, as all the shops were not busy, supplying him the cigarettes which he smoked hurriedly to ask for more.

Everyone knew that he was worthless and harmless in that regard. He had no patience for courtship or a love life. It was never known if he had a relationship with one of the women who laughed at his obscenities.

Given his loud-mouth he was considered incapable of secrecy by most. So the clever people only extracted information about others in the town from him, and never provided him any.

Parmale always talked about his neighbor's wife with a man--and never his own wife. So he never ran into trouble. For his enterprise he demanded a tip often on top of the cigarettes he smoked or the tea he drank, with authority, from a person whom he thus entertained. Mostly he got a few coins. Even if he did not get any he never seemed to mind.

Occasionally he did small but specialized jobs, like white-washing the inner walls made of mud in a house, after bringing the white soil from a distant place only he knew.

At times he was establishing a floor of red clay in a newly-built house, over the wooden flakes. Such jobs were seasonal and mostly he was idle.

The town abounded with houses made by well-cut and arranged stones to make the walls. Those walls were plastered with mud or cement.

Their roofs were made of black, nicely-cut flat stones, which rested on chopped wood, which, in turn, were neatly arranged on the whole trunks of the sal-trees placed over the walls. The roof was built in a way that it slanted on both the sides from its high center.

The flat stones making the roof were cut and arranged neatly to make a design. They made lines crossing each other at precise angles if seen from a distance.

Those houses were well-insulated and lasted for centuries if the wood did not decay or the mud got washed away by the leaking roofs.

Those houses mostly were built by materials locally available during a time when steel or cement were not easily available. They needed a man like Parmale to maintain them.

Parmale charged substantially for his specialized services, which were highly sought after during the Diwali Festival when the people particularly cleaned their houses in that town.

They were shopkeepers mostly and the festival was for appeasing the goddess of wealth Laxmi.

Parmale never rented a room or a sleeping-place in his life. There could be any unused cramped place in a house in the town, which he bartered for bringing water, looking after the children or any other such less rigorous household job, in exchange for a sleeping place for him there.

He strangely ran into problems with his landlords often enough and shifted with his few-belongings bundled in a sheet of cotton from one corner of the town to another. He always criticized his previous house owner but never the current, and got shelter in a house however. At times he returned to a house—to my amusement.

He never ate a meal he did not cook, as he was Brahman. His meals were substantial, as the people, who fed him with a meal, told. It was mandatory to feed him on top of the cash he got as wages when he was working. His meal he cooked himself at the house he was working at, taking a break during the afternoon.

He was small, tender and slim under the cotton kurta, payjama and the boat-shaped cap he always wore. He added a thick, worn-out woolen sweater during winter to his dress.

He always wore rubber-slippers which made a clicking sound while he walked around with his precise steps.

Parmale never made a serious attempt at making a

living. People said it was because of his sad experience with marriage.

At times he left the town and shifted to a village in the neighbourhood, accusing the town-people of being callous, indifferent and greedy. He always returned however, as the jobs there were rigorous and no one had time for his crude jokes. Or was he out-joked there?

There were stories that when he arrived in the town for the first time—recently deserted by his wife and still in his teens—people noticed him running from one end of bazaar to the other only wearing his underwear. His body was covered with ash and sandalwood paste marked his forehead, chest and limbs.

Later it was known that, the contractor of renown of the town, who was building roads, to connect it to a bigger town, had promised him a job, in exchange for the show.

Parmale never got the job from that contractor. But he never lost his touch afterwards and remained a distinguished entity in the town. Almost a celebrity he was considered to be.

Recently I heard that he died after a brief illness in one of the houses he returned to. It made me sad. But thinking about his jokes I smiled. I always thought that, in his heart, he was a simple and innocent person. I was glad that he did not suffer much in the end, in spite of his loneliness.

Living with Karma

'Have you heard Didi that our Thuldidi – (the eldest sister) – has died?' asked her sister, who was the youngest among the three sisters and two brothers. Both were widows of retired army men surviving on pensions of their late husbands, beyond the age of seventy.

Her younger sister lived in a village a little distance away from the town where she lived. In that town pensions were distributed through a branch of a government-owned bank to mostly retired army men or their widows who lived in many nondescript villages in the neighbourhood. There were very few other jobs for the employees of the bank in that town, which remained overcrowded on almost all working days. So most customers of the bank were pension drawers.

Her sister, after the death of her husband, walked for two hours to reach the town to withdraw money from her pension account. Earlier she came twice a year mostly – but more frequently if there was a pressing need. Thus the widowed sisters met more often now then ever before, after their childhood marriages. Their father used to say that delaying the marriage of a girl after she has reached menstruation was against what is prescribed in the religion. So all three sisters were married off as soon they entered their teens.

Recently road has reached her sister's village too, and she rode in a bus to the town now. Now she came almost every other month. She liked to visit the town and her sister there.

She always arrived before the bank-hour started with gifts like fruits or vegetables she grew in the small farm at her village. This time she had brought a few pieces of reddish-brown coloured radish with its green leaves intact.

The tuber part of it was used as salad and the leaves were cooked to make vegetable. However, she was not as generous as her sister. She seldom offered her anything more than a cup of tea when she returned after withdrawing pension from the bank to say her goodbye.

The town had many shops and their owners and their dependents. They all lamented the paucity of business on every occasion they met. Mostly the pensioners were the customers of those shops, apart from a few on-leave soldiers.

Few people from those villages neighboring the town ever got educated enough to find any other kind of job. Those, who proved exceptional, permanently migrated to different cities.

The people once rejected from joining the army, therefore, had no choice but to stay in their villages and make a living through poorly rewarding agriculture. They applied methods in farming which have remained unchanged for centuries.

No one was ever reported to have tried innovations to improve the productivity, though the state-owned TV ran agriculture related programs throughout the evening almost every day between the irregular power-supply which silenced the TV often. People checked often with the TV as the programme with cinema songs was to follow the agricultural-one.

This time too her sister hurriedly went to the bank after leaving her with the radish pieces. It gave her enough time to hide the packets of sweets her step son has brought to celebrate the Diwali festival.

He had come to see her and his stepbrother. Earlier one of her step sons came to see them every year after their father died a few years ago at the ripe age of nearly eighty and she too became a pension-drawing widow. But they came less often as the time passed.

The mother of her stepsons, or the second wife of her husband, had died nearly thirty years ago by drowning in the river in the backyard of their house where she went for a daily bath in the morning before she started her day with a Puja — leaving behind her two infant sons.

After her death she returned to stay with her husband and her step sons from her parents' home.

It was considered dishonourable for a woman who has been married off to return to live at her parents' home called *Maiti*. She could not raise any of the many children she delivered as her husband was often away at his army job. It rendered her bitter and ill-mannered and her husband abandoned her.

When her husband married for the second time she could not protest and instead went to her *Maiti* to live, thinking that she will never live with her husband again.

In the meanwhile the second wife of her husband gave birth to two sons. But after her sudden death she was living with him again after nearly a decade. She became pregnant once again and delivered a son in her forties. But her son turned out to be a mentally-invalid boy.

She raised him along with her motherless step sons. Her step sons grew-up and went to colleges as the years went by. Then they found jobs in a distant city and got married and had children.

But their earnings were just enough to sustain their wives and children. They left their step mother and their invalid step brother with the pension of their father in the house their father built in the town.

They both intended to settle permanently in the city and were desperately trying to muster the money for it.

Her stepson saw her hiding the packets of sweets under a cot. On the three cots in the room beds was laid to sleep-on only and on waking were neatly folded on one side – like in an army-barrack.

It left the string made cots naked or covered with a jute-sack or a worn out army-blanket only. On asking, to his surprise, his stepmother told that she was hiding those sweets' packets from her sister. He just smiled on it.

Her sister returned from the bank with a few packets of biscuits she had purchased for her mentally-invalid, now middle-aged, nephew – who always got a special attention from every visitor for his invalidity. She looked much older than her elder sister in her white cotton dhoti of a widow and her opaque eyes.

Maybe she was tired due to the stress of making

the journey. There was a strange unpleasant smell around her, of unwashed body fluids, secreted possibly in old age. Then she broke the news of the death of their *Thuldidi*.

'Oh! ...I never heard the news,' replied his stepmother, 'When did it happen?'

'It was only a month ago. A woman from my village came from her Maiti with this news. Else I might have not known it. In fact, I wanted to come to you earlier to give this news but it was because of my pregnant buffalo that I got delayed.'

Both sisters wept for a while in the memory of their eldest sister, and their toothless, wrinkled faces seemed older.

'Didi do you remember that our *Thuldidi* was sent away in the *Jhakula* (A type of skirt), for a small amount to her future husband who was still an infant. Later she made rounds around the sacred fire behind her husband in his house, after she started menstruating, graduating formally to become his wife. Only then she began wearing a Dhoti from *Jhakula*.'

'Yes... How can I forget that *Bahini*? She never visited her *Maiti* afterward. She always was too angry to be sold away like that. Only the very poor, who could not feed their daughters, sent them away like that in a marriage, only for a paltry-sum, sometimes to a much older husband. Or often, to the one, who was marrying for the second or the third time, in those days.

'You know being born as a girl is like losing out on your Karma Bahini! During those days only the well-to-do people donated their daughters through a Kannyadan in a marriage from their own homes—only after they had started menstruating and were wearing a dhoti. Being given away in a *Jhakula* to her husband even before a girl is menstruating and for some money was very insulting for a girl. It was like selling an animal. We both were lucky in that regard, as our brothers got recruited in the army soon after our *Thuldidi* was married off and we were donated respectably to our husbands through a Kannyadan. Poor girl... Our *Thuldidi*... she suffered the most!'

More tears were being shed by the sisters.

'Thankfully, our *bhinaju* was a cultured man. He treated her well and was enamoured of the beauty of our *Thuldidi*. Else she might have suffered more. You can not deny that our *Thuldidi* was the most beautiful girl in the area, as everybody said,' she added finding no response from her younger sister.

'But these days *didi* that tradition has disappeared. Even the poor people do Kanyadan and marry-off their daughters with a dowry, instead of taking money from the grooms like before. You know how much in debt I am after marrying-off my two granddaughters?' her sister finally said.

'Yes I know *bahini*... Our poor old *Thuldidi*... She suffered the most. Now she is no more. Did her sons perform the proper rites when she died?' asked the elder sister.

'Yes they did. I hear her sons and grandsons are richer than you and me. They run a very successful business in a distant city. They looked after her very well till the end. Now her husband is alone in the village. I hear that they are taking away him to the city soon.

'*Didi* since we too are quite old now, I do not know how long we shall live! I have crossed seventy years recently and you are older to me. Every time I meet you these days I think if it could be the last,' the younger sister said and started to weep loudly. She was consoled by the elder one.

'*Bahini*, you have so many grand-children to look after you. My stepsons are always away. I do not know what will happen to me. You see my own son is *lata* (a dumb). What he will do if I fall sick? Who will do my last rites, when I die?'

'In that regard your stepsons are very gentle. They always come to see you. I am sure they will look-after you and do the rites after you die. After all, everybody knows how well you raised them after their mother died. They have to live in this society only, so they have to fulfill the obligations of their family. They can not leave you alone. Here... I have brought a few biscuits for your *lata*.'

'Oh... Why you spent so much money? I forgot to ask you but did you have food in the morning or not? Or I will prepare you a meal right away with the leaves of the radish you have brought and will make a few rotis. My step son has also brought some *ghee* (butter) for celebrating Diwali,' the elder sister said.

'No *didi*... Don't bother for me! I always have my meal in the morning after I prepare it, and have only one meal a day.'

'Then let me make you some tea. You stay here in the sun and talk to my *lata*, though he rarely understands anything or replies. God knows what I would be doing if I did not have him to talk to. What will happen to him when I die? I have asked so many people, but no one wants to give away his daughter to marry my *lata*...

'Had it been the earlier days, I could have easily bought a bride for him. I think, though he is a *lata*, he is capable of producing a son. We would have worked to raise his family. His father tried to find a wife for him until his very last. But he couldn't.

'*Bahini* just watch-out for a poor family which has too many daughters to marry! I will approach them to get my *lata* a wife. As you know both of my stepsons are away with their families in the city... They have to... What they would do here otherwise? There is hardly any business here. But they come to see me often. I am happy with that.'

'What to do *didi*... We have to live with our Karma. But last time you declined the proposal for your son's marriage I brought. It was of the girl who was educated till she failed in the SLC exams--only because she was a lame. You said how you could look-after two invalid people at your age. Finding a healthy bride for your son is difficult. Still I shall try.

I have to look after my daughter-in-law and grandsons too. My son, though he does some job in the city, has taken a second-wife there. He never sends any money. We grow some fruits and vegetables to survive. My grandson comes to this town to sell them. Has he not come here to see you ever?'

'Yes, he came here last time with a few green bananas, and took away without asking me an electronic watch I purchased for my *lata* for forty rupees. Though my *lata* does not know how to read the watch, he always insisted on buying him one.'

'He might have. He was showing it to me a few months ago. When I asked him from where he got the watch, he did not tell. But anyway, he is also your grandson. You know his elder brother is a police officer and got a medal recently for shooting two Maoists dead recently, when they tried to snatch away his gun finding him alone. People say he will rise in his job.'

'Yes, that is right. Now you wait here until I make the tea.'

Muse: The Casualty

"I know you guys are always trying to 'Press-the-panic-button'; to try to 'Pull-the-rug-from-under-others', instead of focusing on increasing your sales," Kailas said often nowadays, while in office, and talking to his underlings – between a few other words he uttered in English.

He returned to the local language soon, which everyone in the office understood better. Such English phrases as he often used he picked-up from a business magazine subscribed by his office. This magazine he ignored earlier but had started reading recently.

Those phrases percolated down the hierarchy in the office, which ended in a peon.

The monthly business magazine appeared on a glossy paper often with an interview of the owner of a company as its cover story. There were glittering photographs of his family between the pages full of advertisements of the products of that company.

The businessman interviewed always dropped hints at the contribution of his wife in making him a successful man. It was a cue which the interviewer repeatedly refused to take by not asking the industrialist any question about his wife or in-laws.

In spite of the European-educated economists, lamenting about the things going from 'bad-to-worse' in their newspaper columns, the business-magazine never failed to reward the top five businessmen every year in a glittering ceremony in a five-star hotel. This event was sponsored by different companies and attended by their owners, executives and the invited media persons. There were also present a few leading politicians and stars from show business and cricket in the event. They all talked about achieving excellence.

The event was widely reported in the media the next day, thanks to the lavish food and drinks offered there to the attending media persons. 'Event-management' has started to emerge as a major subject for the aspiring students in a university, to study, by now.

Last time, when the business-magazine presented the interview of the owner of his company as its cover-story, Kailas got five-hundred copies of it from his company. They were meant to be distributed among his friends and relations. Most copies were still lying undistributed at his apartment.

There were photographs of the fat and ugly children of the owner of his company in that issue of the magazine, on a more glossy paper than a cine-magazine.

In fact, many of the cine-stars were being hired to present a show at the marriage ceremony in a businessman's family nowadays, as the cine-industry was not doing so well. This trend perhaps caught-up after Michael Jackson presented a dance on a birthday of the Sultan of Brunei.

The element of family was always present around. A cine-star's children turned out to be cine-stars only, and a musician's children were always the musicians. However the casualty was often the muse of their creations.

Even a pathologist's son turned-out to be a pathologist only, to inherit the modern-pathological lab his father has amassed over the years while peeping into that darned microscope.

Then there was the story of the 'Egyara-Bist' who was a retired armyman. His eleven sons, those he produced out of his two wives, joined the army after dropping-out from school one after another. He had outlived some of his sons though the 'Egyara-bist' died recently. The supply of army-rum at his home, fabulously, never dwindled ever for his guests.

The people who resented you dropped the hints at the lesser family you belonged to, or, are related to. And the people who liked you scanned for the possibilities if you had a family relation with them.

You ran into a family-politics often, no matter where you went or who you worked with. The rulers or the influential people talked as if the politics of their family is the politics of the nation and of the world.

They referred to their family members with their family names in their talks, making it incumbent on their interlocutors to know who they were talking about. And also, who-is-where in the hierarchy of their family — with his or her family name. I mean who is the most and the least favoured by them.

If you too were good at it you also manipulated the circumstances and the people and made a career for yourself. Or you became the casualty of the family politics of others. You always contributed to the institution of family, however, in any case.

"Focus on your sales, and make sure that you earn the incentives this year," Kailas said. The phrases he picked-up, mercifully, lost their currency before long—to the newer ones.

He had made his way up in the hierarchy of the company. Earlier he slept in a dormitory with a common latrine and an open-air bath, near the hand-pump — when he went on an official tour.

He had grown to his present status of a General Manager in one of the many divisions of the company. But, under his shirt, his vest was ridden with as many tiny holes as ever and the elastic of his sock never held its ground.

He, however, often boasted of his having finally been arrived, to his underlings, while narrating his story of success in his company.

He claimed that his daughter never switched-off the air conditioner at his home in Delhi even during the winter, though she used many blankets to sleep. Delhi's winter could be as cold as it is in the hills though its summer is very hot, as the city is near to the desert of Rajasthan. Kailas wanted, among other things, to communicate that, he had enough power to run the air-conditioner non-stop, while most of the people do not have power more than half the time in Delhi.

He went no more to the small nondescript towns with irregular electric-power supply, by a rickety bus, which plied the dusty roads. Instead he landed in a city to check into a reserved-room at a five-star hotel.

He ate enough of the complimentary breakfast though, at the five-star hotel, to never need a lunch – for which he had to pay from his own pocket and as his allowances were fixed. He had his dinner at a street corner eatery like before where the working people on-tour, who lived in a dormitory, like he did before, also came to have their dinner. Many of them who knew him talked about his unchanged simple ways inspite of his spectacular rise in his company for eating the same dinner while on tour.

He returned to the five-star hotel to sleep and have the complimentary breakfast the next day.

Meanwhile the tightness of his body has given way to the middle-heavy type, while his hair thinned and turned grey. The centre of gravity now was between his big belly and massive butt.

Ill-fitting pants held in place by a broad leather steel-buckled belt; and a tight half-sleeved, hairy-arms-revealing cotton shirt, emblazoned by an atrociously-coloured Chinese-tie, tucked into his belly by a free tie-pin covered his undulating body while he was in his office on a working day now.

The tiny beard he grew in half-grey, below his lower lip and above the chin under his randomly truncated moustache, created a deadly effect. His smile now made him look a bigger crook than he actually was, revealing a copper false-tooth on the front.

The only false tooth in his mouth replaced the genuine one he had lost while commuting on his duty, in a city in the south, and met an accident, when he was in a junior position. It was considered a testimony to the many sacrifices he had made for the company, while climbing-up in the hierarchy of it.

Kailas particularly resented the General Manager of another division of his company, who was also a relative of the owner of the company. Though equally graying like him he was not fattening--unlike him-- and always had a playful smile on his clean-shaven face. It made him look much younger than Kailas.

He sat in a cabin at the entrance of the office facing three young lady-receptionists, sitting across the glass window of his cabin, and keeping an eye on everyone who entered or left the office through another glass-window. Kailas had his cabin at the end of the office.

All the other male underlings working in that office, some of them were much younger and good-looking than both the GMs, were herded in a hall between the cabins of the two GMs. They faced the passageway closed by a self-closing, creaky, wooden-door. A small window of glass on it gave them a sight of some one passing by the narrow gallery.

They were seated in a way that, from their seats, they could not land an eye on one of the young lady-receptionists, through the glass window. Coming out of the hall, from their seats, entailed opening of the door, which creaked in protest, and self-closed with a thumping sound—inviting many pairs of eyes.

The other GM was always ready to tell stories about the sickness of his wife. He was a mysterious character who always stared at the receptionists when he was free.

The gossip was that he was instead an ailing person and not his wife, and due to the diabetes he had, he was almost impotent. His taste for pleasure in life could not be denied however, as he was always ready to discuss the efficacy of the medicines meant for increasing the sexual potency ranging from Viagra to *Shilajit*.

Such kind of advantageous circumstances for his rival, in the company, made Kailas look sadder. He knew that his rival will get any chance of promotion over him for being a relation of the owner of the company.

He resented being in his office from where he could look only at the backyard of the building. To get out of it he was often on tour, staying in the five-star hotels and eating the complimentary breakfasts to gain more weight.

These circumstances also made him look older. He

was always on the lookout for an issue to come up, that he could take up with one of his subordinates, in his thin whining voice.

His small, grey patch of beard under his lip and above his chin made him look comical, instead of threatening. Every time he shouted at a subordinate others in the office secretively smiled at his voice, for it was not so befitting a man of his size and weight. The stiff exchange of pleasantries between the two GMs created a curious-scene, whenever they met. It made the other staff giggle.

The underlings reporting to both GMs were aware that the real power was with the one who was a relation of the owner of the company. So the smiling type of the GM was more feared in the office, than the shouting one.

No one among them ever was seen making advances towards any of the three woman receptionists, though the latter at times could be seen trying to court a young man from among the staffs. The man being courted mostly hesitated to respond, as there was the fear of inviting the hostility of the smiling GM.

Memories of Nasbandi Days

Nasbandi, as vasectomy was called there, was a word much-feared, during the 'emergency' days in India, more than a quarter of a century ago. Not only so in the Indian side, but also in bordering towns on the Nepalese side as well. There were legion stories related to NB widely circulated among the people on either side. Some of them were tragic, like the one of a Nepalese teen-aged boy, who went in search of a job in the neighbouring Indian town. Things transpired in a way that he ended-up receiving a NB.

He returned to his home broken both physically and psychologically. He never married afterwards, and runs a small teashop at the border nowadays. At the insistence of his customers he still repeats his story which the people listen with rapturous attention, between the sips of tea, at his shop. He no more seems to harbour rancour about the tragic incident.

Then there was the funny story of a Nepalese trader, who used to conduct his business of trading in goods across the border. He naturally had good relations with the police and custom officials on either side of the border – as without it, his trade would not have been viable. He proudly rode his horse on both the sides of the border, which he needed to cross almost every day in the course of carrying out his business. Horses were the only alternative mode of transport in those days, in the hills, and keeping one was considered a matter of prestige – just like owning a car nowadays.

One day he returned home on his horse looking a little less proud than usual. On inquiring by a friend he told that for some time he has decided to give-up his business, as a police-officer on Indian side was putting pressure on him to receive a NB operation. He also told that the government servants on the other side were expected to arrange a certain number of cases of NB, to save their jobs. The trader was incredulous that the police-officer would put pressure on him as well, to have a NB operation, as he was a regular source of bribe for him. More so, when everyone knew that he recently had married for the second time – after his first wife had proved a barren.

Also heard was that, in the town – on other side of the border – the school kids were asked by their teachers to put pressure on their father – to have a NB. Everyone there suspected and speculated that his neighbour was the most recent case (of receiving the NB operation).

In fact, many such rumours did the rounds on both the sides. There were some true-stories as well. Like the one of a psychologically-depressed man, who was a father of five children at a very early age, during the days when very few people had the concept of contraception. A condom really was a curious thing to make jokes about, or to play volleyball with, during the Holi Festivals, in those days. Though the government persistently promoted 'The red triangle' in India, which was the symbol of family planning.

It was a credulous time when many of the people believed that the children were gifts of God, rather than the result of the fulfillment of carnal desires of men and women. The man in question received his NB operation as bliss and went on to become a womanizer afterwards. As per the folklore, his sterilization was his USP for seduction in most of the cases. The man still lives to this day and cracks dirty-jokes with the enthusiasm and recklessness of an adolescent.

There was another tale of a person who actually was the butt of jokes among his pals for fathering a child almost every year out of his two wives. However, he always complained that he had a progressively-deteriorating eyesight needing a change of lenses frequently.

In fact, he received his NB very thankfully indeed and no more fathered more children. There were many other, equally intriguing stories in the following years. Like the one of the birth of children to the wives of the people who had, reportedly, received the NB operation.

People speculated that the operation failed in such instances, while others – particularly the neighbours--argued that the matters were not so simple.

Today, when the politicians on either side of the border routinely stress that the people of both the countries share a unique and common cultural heritage, one cannot help but recall these stories, among other things. These stories were of the people on either side of the border, and became a part of folklore--on both the sides.

Nowadays, more than a quarter-century later, the generation of people who received the NB operation is slowly depleting, and these stories are nearly forgotten. Thankfully, the 'Emergency' did not last too long in India, and an entirely different type of personality became the next prime minister—replacing Indira Gandhi.

It is another matter that his peculiar habit of drinking his own urine became the fresh source of rumour and humour on both the sides of the border. The whole world has indeed undergone a sea-change since then. Looking back to those days still may bring smile to ones face.

A Meeting of Cultures

(One)

Like us, she had not taken the availability of sun for granted. I realised it while translating in English the process of pickling lemons, which my wife was explaining in Nepali. She asked in her heavy, German-accented English, which entailed a frequent clicking sound of the tongue, how the lemon could be pickled if the sun is not available for weeks at a stretch, as was the need.

I was taken aback by it. After thinking for a while I said that, maybe she could use oven at a low temperature to season the pickle in the absence of sun. Then she asked if the taste of oven-seasoned lemon pickle would be the same, as at our home. I had no answer to it. Like for other things we cooked and offered her to eat at our home when she came to visit us, she made a note of the process and ingredients in her notebook.

She said certain spices she took with her to cook Nepali-style meal in Germany and she used chopsticks to eat at home, instead of a spoon. Like me she was a vegetarian. She had problems in finding proper food here, as the meat of buffalo is popular in Kathmandu, and costs a fifth only than the castrated male-goat's meat.

Buffalo-meat dumplings served in Kathmandu eateries her brother liked very much, when he came to visit her. For vegetarians getting an uncontaminated food has remained a problem here. My wife on occasions cooked fish for her. She had developed a taste for milk tea as is prepared here, and also had it there in Germany—she said. She often asked how good quality tea-leaves could be identified and found. We had tea always but were not particular about its different brews. So her questions often illuminated how ritual even our mundane activities were.

I never saw her taking alcohol, though she said she had wine at times at her home. She said she went to a party on a bicycle, so that she could return pulling it if she got drunk, and she never drove a vehicle after drinking.

Though on the day of Shiv-ratri (the birth day of Lord Shiva), she had a piece of sweet mixed with cannabis leaves with me, as the festival is celebrated here in this manner. Cannabis is considered to be the favourite drug of Shiva, who took this herb to keep him entertained in the loneliness of living in the Himalayas, or so the myths are about him.

But cannabis is illegal otherwise here. So the culture is at odds with the legal system here, in this regard. However, it has been already legalized in certain civilized countries in the West. May be they will be decriminalized here too, as they are possibly not more dangerous than alcohol or tobacco, the drugs the governments allows to consume mostly and benefits from, by taxing them, almost everywhere.

My wife was watching us while we took those sweets, as she did not take such things like cannabis. We waited then for the kicks to arrive. It never happened however. I wondered if due to the high demand during Shivratri, by the Sadhus, who arrive in Kathmandu from faraway places, to take a Darshan of Pashupatinath, that cannabis went in short supply. Hence the confectioners made the sweets with other green leaves, leaving the Bhakts like us high and dry.

Some Indian Sadhus the next day complained about the scarcity or low quality of 'booty' in Kathmandu, while they spoke to a local TV news-channel at the bus park. They were returning back after celebrating Shivratri in Kathmandu. In the morning only they were provided with a little cash in an envelope as 'Dakshina' by the government of Nepal. Even after the country had been declared a republic and secular one this Hindu tradition is maintained by the government. The Dakshina also was seldom to their satisfaction, as some of them complained that it was not sufficient even for covering their travel expenses.

How much she cherished the sun had become apparent to us before too. It was the beginning of a spring here. The shoots of green in the pomegranate tree in our compound declared it, though the air was still cold in the absence of sun. The blighted-tree even flowered and fruits appeared later, as she happily pointed out, as it turned into a summer and she kept on visiting us. She said how pleasant it was, when the season changes, recalling how the tree looked like, during autumn to her, sitting similarly on the same chair in our apartment.

We did not tell her that the fruits of the tree decayed and dropped, as soon the monsoons arrived. Our landlord had once explained to us that the disease of that pomegranate tree was treatable with certain chemicals. But he did nothing about it. It was for about a decade now that we have been witnessing the flowering of the tree and the dropping of its rotten fruits, just as they were about to ripen, every year. Meanwhile, our infant first son became an adolescent and we had a second-son too.

Trying to raise a family consumes your time and energies so totally that only others are able to see the years past in your life, marked often by the appearance of wrinkles on your face, or by the graying of hair.

One even fails to see the passing-years even in the growth of his children -- which had to be pointed out by others as well. Only while referring to old-photographs, that you become aware of the time that has gone-by. Only a good-time could have passed so unnoticed, as the bad times hardly go away early enough, and leave behind unpleasant memories.

My wife met her when she joined a private school offering training in fashion-designing and tailoring. She was also attending it. But she argued a lot with the people in the management, and the teachers, as the things were running in a less than perfect manner in that school.

Often there were absent teachers or other

logistical problems. The school was owned by a successful
ladies-tailor of Kathmandu, who was recently ailing with
a nervous degenerative disease.

The deficiencies at the school were too much for
her to bear. When its management offered her excuses —
like the domestic problems of the individuals running it,
or the sickness of its owner — to cover them, she became
furious on it.

The school was situated on the outskirts of the
city. She soon dropped-out without asking for any refunds.
My wife, though, completed the course to get a
certificate and open her own boutique shop. It was
something our relatives frowned upon, arguing that
tailoring did not go properly with our higher Hindu-caste.
We pacified them by saying that it was not tailoring but
fashion-designing, which is considered a well-respected
profession globally. My wife and the German woman became
close friends.

(Three)

Sunlight entered into our bedroom through a big window at
a slanting angle during the winter afternoons. The face
of the person sitting on the chair near the tailoring-
machine, next to the window, glinted in the light.

Sun had become intense now and we knew that soon
it will enter into our room, in the coming months, from a
straighter angle. My wife dropped the curtains to avoid
the sun.

Her German friend however, always insisted on
keeping them open, so that the sun fell directly on her
face and open shoulders, while she tried to practice the
skills she had learnt at the school, looking at the
pomegranate tree and beyond. She reminded us that she had
to return home soon and during March also it is about
minus five degree Celsius there, at times, in northern-
Germany.

We never believed her when she said that she never
liked her country and family. Quarrels broke out often
between her parents and her granny. The German people

were the unhappiest according to her.

I reminded her that it happens everywhere in a family and it was a comfort that they were all living-together in a house — three generations of her family. She agreed and said that very few of her friends back home had their parents living together. I also told her that, as I recently knew through the DW TV, in Munich, a big hall has been built with an artificial sun. People could go there and feel like being in sun for a fee, with the artificially created light and heat. She welcomed the news.

After meeting her I became more interested in German matters and gathered my information from TV channels and other sources. The coverage of European cultural matters on DW TV I still like a lot. It is very different than what the BBC and CNN have to offer.

When I asked her and her brother — who had come to visit her for a few weeks — who they thought were the most influential Germans, their first guess was Hitler.

His name they uttered with a little rejection, looking at each other. When I said that they were Bismarck, Goethe, and Karl Marx, in that order, as I had learnt recently — they became a little surprised. Her refrain often was that the people in Germany were very lazy and thought as if the whole world only spoke the German language.

I had to often remind her about the great cultural and industrial development Germany has made. I offered her jokingly, to exchange our nationalities, if she disliked her country so much. She just smiled, on it.

She had been here for the past whole year, she said. Twice before too she came here. In-between she went to China, and worked in a farm in Spain for some time, and had lived in the USA and England too, for some time. French people were happier than German — she informed.

The EU was expanded to twenty-five members, while we were watching it live on TV that day. She was skeptical, and said the German people will lose jobs that way; and she complained that the ceremony was taking place using the English language only.

She asked if the BBC was a British TV channel. English people, she said, talked to you when they needed to, and stopped the communication when they did not like anything of it. They even closed their country too when they felt so. British culture she did not like much--she said. She laughed when I explained to her how a clock is different from a watch.

Her brother lived in South-America, whenever he could. She said the unemployment- allowances were about seven hundred Euros a month in her country, which her brother came to collect in Germany, before he returned to the Latin America again. It would not be so forever and soon her brother will have to take up a job, she told. She smiled when I suggested that why would someone do a job and not remain unemployed in her country.

She avoided talking about the politics of Nepal and always went back to cultural topics. She dyed her hair black – though I pointed out that the people here changed to golden, which she had hid.

She said she wanted to look like a Nepali woman as it helped in avoiding unnecessary attention. The charges here were as high as ten US dollars for foreigners, just to enter some archaeological sites in Kathmandu. She knew many back-door entries to such sites, where there was no surveillance to single-out the foreigners.

I welcomed her cheating of a cheating system. She said in her country too the things are not very difference that way.

She complained however, about the way smiling men discreetly touched her without saying anything directly, while she used the crowded public-transport system of the city – taking her for a Nepali girl. She indeed looked a charming Nepali woman with her thin and delicately framed body of an average height and her dyed black hair falling on her forehead, easily tempting a Nepali man to make advances.

She resented the way they were made, however. One day, while she was having tea at a stall, after dinner, a few chaps tried to harass her.

She was very angry at that incident. 'Why should

someone impose on her against her wishes?', she asked. She said she was free to go wherever she liked and at whatever time she preferred.

Her brother was taller than six feet and younger by nearly a decade to her, and had golden-blonde hair falling on his shoulders. With a rubber-band he tied them often, making a ponytail. He spoke a much better English and was well-versed in various issues including politics. He said that he opted for English and her sister for Russian, as an optional language at the school, and they belonged to East-Germany before.

He said he studied Geology and her sister studied Journalism in the university. Either military or civil service was mandatory for German citizens, for a minimum of two-years. He had served that tenure in the civil, as he disliked the army. They said women were excluded from this provision of the mandatory service of the government. When I asked why should there be positive-discrimination for the fairer-sex, they became startled.

She meditated and did a lot of reading in her moderately-priced hotel room, where she stayed for months, whenever she came here. She felt safe there as everybody of the hotel-running family treated her well. She went for morning walks to Swaymbhunath every day. Hiking those countless steps to reach the top of the hillock where the dome of the monastery was situated was her favourite activity.

She stayed here to do it throughout the year was surprising to me – since we made a living with so much efforts and remained ever preoccupied with it alone-- she took living almost for granted. My questions about her country and life there kept on growing. She ignored most of them, for often there was a problem when she tried to explain something in English. I was happy to know whatever she told and explained the same to my wife too.

Some things my wife could not understand about her culture. They communicated even when I was not around and my wife could barely speak any intelligible English. They smiled and laughed about things while whatever communication they could manage. She said she tried to

learn Nepali too but abandoned as things did not go well
– as with her tailoring school. She had a profound
knowledge about the cultural celebrations taking place in
Kathmandu Valley, at different times of the year.

The city consists of numerous old towns – now
being bridged by newly constructed modern buildings – and
various cultural and ethnical groups, not to mention the
castes and the sub-castes. There were numerous festivals
which were celebrated by the people living in Kathmandu.
She calculated the precise dates of those occasions
through a Nepali calendar and participated in all of them
by reaching the venue when she was here.

Those celebrations taking place during a night she
attended with her Nepali-boyfriend, at times staying out
for the whole night. Once she surprised me by sending
greetings on a Nepali Festival of Dashain, which is
calculated as per the lunar calendar, from Germany by
email.

She said she rarely had visited the 'freak-street'
of Kathamndu – the Thamel District – popular among other
tourists with its discotheques and the massage parlours.
In Thamel her brother disappeared almost every night when
he was here. There a Hollywood celebrity or a tennis-star
could disappear for weeks before being noticed. Charles
Shovraj, a wanted criminal of Interpol lived in Thamel
for months before he was recognised and was taken into
the custody by police, after a newspaper identified him
and published his pictures. He has been in a jail in
Kathmandu for the past few-years now.

She did not introduce her boyfriend to her brother,
thinking that her brother would not like him. Then they
went out for a week for tracking in the nearby hills. Her
brother said that it was an educational tour for him, as
he was studying Geology. They were apprehensive due to
the escalating Maoist insurgency. They returned safe
however, happier and fitter, to our delight.

Particularly my younger infant son became attached
to her, due to her frequent visits to our home, and asked
frequently for her, when she was away. Soon her brother
returned to Germany and she was alone again. Her brother

did not come to see us for the second time, though we had invited them both.

I wanted to talk about several things with him, as he spoke English very well. During our only conversation he said he liked the Nepali culture and it must be protected from the Western influence. When I asked him how a culture could remain unchanged in progressively worsening living-conditions of its people, he did not answer.

When I said that the people here were hard working and wanted the education and not the alms he became contemplative. His body was thin like his sister's, and he smoked a lot of cigarettes he made from tobacco and papers he always carried with him in a pouch. His features were soft and kind.

With his long-hair he looked like an artist or a painter. We did not meet again to discuss more things.

(Four)

It is now almost two years, since she had left, after postponing her return many times. My younger son no more asks questions about her return. We have been constantly in touch through emails, though. At least twice she was about to return but had to stay due to an examination of her journalism course, or other matters. Things have changed a lot here since then. We shall have a lot to discuss, when we meet, I am sure.

Wannabe Sadhu
And The Elusive Gyan

They were not rich people but there was enough to meet most of their needs. They had land to employ tenant families for cultivation and Bonod's father worked in a junior position in a government office.

His childhood in a conservative Bangali-Brahmin family in a small town a little distance away from Calcutta, with his two brothers and a sister, was generally happy. He was the eldest born to his parents.

Too much attention and love of his mother had turned him into an obstinate adolescent, who domineered over his siblings and tried to defy his father. Whenever his father tried to assert his authority his mother intervened and salvaged his pride. One day he returned home from school when everybody had gone to bed and his enraged father was waiting for him with a stick in his hand.

As soon as his father saw him he lifted the stick and started to beat him without asking anything. He cried loudly inviting his mother to come to his rescue. She left her bed and tried to intervene. His father was really serious that day and warned his wife to stay away or else she could also receive the stick.

It was the first time Binod received a beating like that from his soft-spoken father. He was angered by the helplessness of his mother. He did not go to school the next day and decided to leave home by the evening. After his father went to office his mother came to placate his anger. Her words only infuriated him more and wanted to go away more urgently.

He knew where his mother kept the money she saved from the household expenses. He lifted small amounts from there earlier--just enough to never have been noticed. That day he took all of it and caught the evening train going to Benaras after he reached Calcutta first by another train from his town.

He had decided to become a Sadhu—a saint--and find the Gyan – the wisdom--after he reached Benaras.

But as the night progressed Binod started to realise what he was leaving behind. The thought of his loving parents and brothers and sister came to his mind repeatedly. He knew that they would be very worried by his sudden absence. Also he thought about his own vulnerability as a young boy who had never lived away from his family. It began to make him fearful of the future. Then there was his hurt pride. He knew, more than his father, his mother would be pained by his disappearance. But he is not going to relent easily and return home, he thought, though he was not sure how things might turn out in Benaras.

In a state of confusion his eyes were filled with tears. He wept silently throughout the night. In the poorly-lit train compartment no one could see his tears to console him. He was also doubtful if anybody would care about him weeping. Outside the window the night was dark and he could see nothing.

The train was making the journey at a steady pace, taking him away from his home with the musical clicking of its movement on the tracks. The journey was briefly broken when the train stopped at identical stations in the vast expansion of flat land, which were flooded by blinding lights. Between the vast darkness he was travelling through this sudden stop at a station did not illuminate anything about his future. The unfamiliar land and people added to the mystery of the night.

Next day Binod reached Benaras. It excited him a little and he roamed around in its bazaars and the famous Ghats on the riverbank. He was tired. He sat on the ground near the gate of the temple he was seeing and fell asleep. When he woke up he was very hungery. He bought some food and ate and started to think what to do next. The second night away from his family was ahead of him. On an impulse he thought if he should return home. But he decided against it, thinking that he should try out on sainthood which he had in mind. If it did not work he might think about returning home.

He decided that to become a Sadhu he needed a guru, and to find one he reached a math in the evening, where a famous Guru lived. The Guru was preaching to his followers and he sat among them and listened. He did not leave when other people left when the preaching was over and the Guru retired to his cabin inside the Math. Binod told one of his attendants that he wanted to join the math to become a disciple of the Guru.

He could not reach the guru immediatelty and had to deal with his disciples for several days who took detailed information about him. There were many layers of hierarchy of the disciples around the guru who observed him and took more information from him. Finally he was allowed to see the Guru one morning. The Guru too asked him a few questions about his family and then said he could join the cult he led.

Binod shaved his head that day and took part in a ritual to be initiated into the cult. Guru gave him a garland of Rudrakshya seeds to wear after the ceremony.

In the following weeks Binod listened to the sermons of the Guru very carefully every evening. He found that the Guru said almost the same thing always. Soon he began to lose interest in the things Guru preached. He was devoid of the faith other disciples had in the Guru, who listened to him talking the same things everyday.

He decided to stay however, and underwent the rigours of the life of a disciple. He hoped that the labour he had to put to be a disciple might help him to become a saint. Also he had not done any demanding labour so far at his home. He felt he enjoyed doing it in the Math.

He went away in the morning to beg in the town and deposited the alms he garnered to the cashier of the Math on returning. Then he became busy with cooking for the staff of the Math along with a few other newly recruited disciples like him. After the Guru and his senior staff had their meal it was mid-day. It was time for Binod and other new interns to have their meal.

Guru rested again after meal. It was only in the evening that his audience arrived and he had to preach.

After a brief respite after meal, Binod and other interns had to finish the job of washing utensils and clothes on the ghat next to the Math. They were expected to finish it before the preaching began to join it and listen to the Guru. After the preaching was over and the Guru retired to his cabin the evening meal had to be prepared by them again.

Soon Binod realised that there was not much gyan—the wisdom--to be acquired here and he decided to change the Guru.

He found the similar circumstances prevailing around the new Guru as well, and his shifting of Gurus continued while the gyan remained elusive for the next several months. There were so many Gurus leading their cults and preaching who occupied most of the Maths in Benaras.

From one Guru he ran away one night when a senior disciple of him tried to molest him.

It was almost a year since he left home. Returning home was what he thought about often. The thoughts about his loving mother and quiet father brought tears to his eyes. He thought if his father now looked sadder and became quieter due to his absence on account of his beating. But there was his pride which always restrained him from returning home even in those moments of frailty.

He then decided to be on his own and live in Benaras without the protection of a Guru. He went to beg in the morning and bought food from a hotel from the alms he had received.

He slept in one of the many maths on the ghat. One day he met another wannabe Sadhu of his own age, who also had ran away from his home and had a similar story to tell like his. His name was Raju.

They became friends. They went together to beg and at times cooked their meal in the Math. If Raju cooked he washed and if he cooked the meal Raju washed. Other works too they had divided amongst them to make a kind of partnetship. It continued for a few months like that.

They got soon tired of it and decided to leave Benaras in search of gyan. They left for Haridwar one day. It was a famous religious place near the mountains where pilgrims came from the distant places and where the Gurus were said to be really knowledgeable and learned.

Raju and Binod instantly liked the town for its picturesque surroundings. It had the mighty river Ganga flowing down from lush green mountains in the north which flew and disappeared into the vast plains in the South of Haridwar. The climate here was more pleasant than they had exprienced in Benaras or elsewhere. The mornings were cool and the days were warm and the evevings were balmy.

They tried to find in the beginning when they arrived in Haridwar first a reasonable guru to continue with their quest of becoming a Sadhu with a gyan.

To their surprise, when they met a few, they discovered that here too the Gurus were not different from the ones in Benaras. More so, they were already used to lead an independent life and feared the endless hours of labour they had to put once they join as a disciple a cult. They again decided to go alone without a Guru.

When they resumed their Benaras-lifestyle of independent, teenager, wannabe Sadhus, Binod and Raju were often mocked at by the other senior Sadhus and their disciples who belonged to a cult. They were too young to be considered a Saint or Sadhu to live so independently a seeker's life.

Some of the people among the pilgrims or the shopkeepers, to whom Binod and Raju went to beg, came to know of their story, for they were still children to be taken seriously as seekers. They treated Raju and Binod with empathy and kindness and often advised them to return home to their parents. Binod and Raju simply ignored that advice.

They had a happy time here for the first time since they left their homes. It made them think less about home.

The alms were plentiful due to the kindness of numerous pilgrims and the beauty of the nature was around to be cherished.

They went to the bridge Laxmanjhula in the evenings to enjoy the scene of river Ganga flowing below it. They stayed there until it became dark and the lights of the town got reflected in the waters of the river.

They occasionally went to Rhishikesh to visit which was an even more beautiful town up in the hills in the north, from where River Ganga descended into Haridwar.

Binod and Raju have nearly passed a year here. Fascinated by the beauty of the nature around they failed to notice the time. But once Binod had fever and was in bed for many days. Raju took his care and bought him medicines. As he recovered it began to occur to both of them that it could not continue like this forever. They started to discuss about returning to their families.

One day Raju finally made up his mind and declared that he was returning home. Binod was in tears when he came to see Raju off at the bus station. Raju asked him to join him at his home. Binod declined the invitation but promised that he will visit him at his home some day. He took his address before Raju left.

Binod was alone once again. His recent sickness had made him worried about future. He thought about his home often now. His pride still did not allow him to return though he remembered often his happy days at his home.

One day, while he was begging among the disembarking pilgrims near a bus, someone called his name loudly. He was startled and tried to run away. When he looked behind he saw an elderly couple and two children behind them running toward him. They were calling his name.

Then he recognised them and stopped. They were his uncle, aunt and cousins. His uncle and aunt embraced him as soon they approached him and tears running down their eyes. They told him that his mother became sick after he left home and could never recover fully. Even his father repented beating him, they told Binod. They asked him to immediately return home with them.

Binod became rigid on hearing it and told them

that since he was a Sadhu now returning home was not possible for him. He wanted a more emphatic persuasion before he relented, to return home respectfully. They took him to the hotel they were staying in and begged him for the whole evening to return. They fed him the best food available there in between.

Finally Binod relented, but only after making sure that he would return on his own terms. In his heart he was delighted however, at the turn of events, as it saved him the embarrassment of returning home without being asked.

After almost three years he returned to his family. Everybody was happy to see him. Binod was surprised at how his siblings had grown-up and his parents looked older. His father had connections to make him appear in school leaving certificate exams of class ten, though he left home when he was still in class eight.

Thanks to the tuitions and his hard work, he passed the exams with good marks to enter into a college for higher studies. Over the years he completed his studies and started a professional career in a company as an accountant and got married as well, to a woman his parents had arranged. He now lived away from home with his family in a distant city where the Head Office of his company was situated.

Those three-years away from his family in his young age had taught him a lot and made him a wise man— if not a Saint. He considered those years more valuable than the years he passed in the University. He cared no more about the sarch of gyan. Particularly he resented the Gurus and chased away their disciples who came to him asking for alms.

A Sal Forest

Our religious books have often displayed a remarkable environmental consciousness by preaching ideas like 'Tyakten Bhunjiyatha,' (consume sparingly), nearly half-a-century ago, unlike at present, bothering too much about the environmental issues was not fashionable.

My father, during my last visit to him that autumn, with his familiar and calm story-telling countenance – which always charmed me, as he talked to himself in such moods, trying to explore his perceptions of the world he knew, and put those into words for me; drawing every time he retold a story deeper into his memory of events, places and the people he came across – once again told me a familiar story of his younger days.

I inadvertently looked for inconsistencies in the stories he told again and again. But there were hardly any ever. Only that he went on to elucidate a new event or a character of his story every time he retold it, which became almost a story within the story. It was in order to make me better understand his story and also keep me engaged, in exploring those memories of him. I thought if I was not there as his audience he might have got distracted from his efforts to recall a story.

It was a familiar story that day he told me. Because he had been telling it to me like many other stories since I was young. It also proved to be the last one because he passed away as soon as the spring arrived of a new millennium. I was not around when he died. I had left him behind to seek my life in the job I was doing in the city six months back.

He is not available anymore to go to visit on a leave from my job. It was a thing I always looked upto while waiting for my next holidays. However, I am left with the recurring memory of his serene countenance while he told a story which was often during morning tea or while we were waiting to go to bed after dinner. Besides, of course, so many other memories of him are there to keep me ever thinking about him.

It began after he joined the British Indian Army's Boys' company, during the wonderful days of the early forties. From the hectic routine of the army coming home every year on a two months' leave was a prospect upon which he always looked ahead with fascination and joy.

He had always been a homesick person. Though, he indeed valued the experiences he had gained while working in the army (that later became the Indian Army) for nineteen youthful years of his life, in the same rank. He never accepted a promotion as he was too much of an independent-minded, opinionated person — the kind which is remotely employable except under the dire financial needs.

Also, for taking promotions, he was supposed to undergo certain trainings which denied him his cherished leaves.

At the first available opportunity he opted for the retirement from the army. It was a decision he never regretted. He was confident that he will make a better money in any other job he would undertake as the salary of army job was too low for him. Besides he was still in his mid thirties when he retired. He said since he was a good shot in bringing down fruits from a tree with a stone in his childhood, he was condident of making the amount of his last salary fall from the sky by throwing stones at it.

During his service years he travelled across the Indian subcontinent extensively and even to (then) Burma, during the Second World War — to fight against the occupying Japanese army.

During this period he acquired a German made lantern with a Belgian made glass having a 'swastika' mark and symbol of crossed flags on it. It also had a serial number. This souvenir still survives in our family home and functions well when the power supply is interrupted almost every evening, nowadays.

It however, lit all the evenings of my childhood days, which were made lively by the stories my father told, as then the electric power had not come to the town.

As soon as my father's company reached Rangoon after travelling for many days in a ship from Medaras they heard that the World War II was over. So he did not get a chance to get involved in the real action.

My father finally retired with an 'exemplary' ranking in the 'character' column of his discharge certificate, in 1961. It was five years before I was born.

However, to reach home, until a few years before his retirement, he had to walk for three days from the nearest railway station. A mule he hired carried his luggage.

The rainy season was not considered particularly good for commuting in that area, as in that leech-infested Ghorato Bato (a horse track), landslides were common.

In fact, the track on which my father walked across was the same on which the famous English hunter Jim Corbett also walked at the beginning of the last century. Jim Corbett, however, did so while he followed the man-eating tigers of Kumaun, Purnagiri or Talladesh. Those beasts he finally killed, before he described his thrilling hunting adventures in his world famous books.

The place where he killed the man-eater of Purnagiri is mentioned on a yellow coloured board of cement in black letters, as it falls near the road of the present day. This road has reduced that three days' walk my father undertook so often into a six hours' bus journey.

The buses stop there allowing the passengers to take a break. The message on the board remains largely ignored however, as a few people are able to read English and those who can read it are seldom interested in the message written on the yellow board near the road.

Even during those days my father noticed that the forests were depleting very fast while observing his surroundings tracking in those remote hills of Kumaun (now in India).

My father decided that something must be done about it. He planned to grow and protect a vanishing forest of sal (maple) trees in our village, with the help of the fellow villagers. One day, during one of his cherished two months' leave, he called a meeting of the fellow-villagers and told them about his intentions. To his pleasure, most of them supported his idea.

He suggested that apart from the house-building needs of the villagers only not a single sal tree shall be axed. My father further proposed that even the 'Dhami' of the village would not be allowed to sell sal trees to the outsiders. He was a hereditary priest at our village temple.

The neighbouring villages were already deficient in sal trees due to their indiscriminate falling. The log of sal tree was considered particularly good for house-building as it lasted for many generations. Also for furniture-making it was a preferred choice of most due to its durability.

The 'Dhami' of our village was a cunning guy. He used to make a lot of money by selling the sal trees of our village to outsiders. To those fellow-villagers who cared or dared to question his arcane enterprise he used to beguile them by saying that whatever he was doing was the will of the God – as he was the representative of the God in our village – being the hereditary priest at the village temple.

'Dhamis' have a great influence on the villagers of the area even to this day. Villagers go to them for a treatment if they suffer from any physical or spiritual problems. 'Dhamis' have political connections too in many cases. Some of them decreed their fellow-villagers to vote in favour of the King's rule, nearly thirty-years ago, in the last political referendum, in which the multiparty choice was defeated by a mere one percent of the vote.

Since those were the innocent times of nearly half-a-century ago the villagers either believed the 'Dhami' or were too afraid of God to further question the motives of the Dhami when he axed a *sal* tree.

My dad was convinced that it was the 'Dhami's' enterprise which was the major reason behind the vanishing forests, not only in our village but also in the neighbouring-ones as well.

The 'Dhami' however, protested vehemently to my dad's proposals and threatened that the wrath of the god would unleash on my father if he interfered in his 'divine' business.

Unperturbed, my dad told him that he was ready to face even god's anger for a public cause. My father strongly believed that – with its environmental value – the sal forest, once created, would become an asset for the posterity. Also, toward that end, pre-empting the cunning designs of crooks like Dhami was an imperative.

My father, after tackling the tantrums of 'Dhami', asserted further with more proposals to the – by now easily acquiescing--fellow-villagers.

He proposed that no one would harvest firewood from the area where he intended to grow the forest. Also, none of the women of the village would bring sal-leaves to feed their cattle from the protected area and, no one among the villagers would send his cattle to graze in that area.

Villagers reluctantly agreed to my father's these proposals, as they were likely to affect their practices of using *sal* products in various ways.

However, once the things were agreed upon my father ensured that they were effectively implemented as well. He made several tentative teams of villagers to check the *goth* or *khark* (rooms to keep the cattle) of every villager. It was to ensure that no one had violated the agreed proposals. He, during his yearly leaves, used to check himself every *goth* and *khark* of the village with torch in his hand, every evening. It all was to make sure that his plan worked.

This plan was effectively implemented for nearly a decade, with the help of the understanding villagers. Those who dutifully, even in the absence of my dad (while he was away for the army duty) made sure that the sal trees of the area remained well-protected.

So nearly one decade of the hard work and vigilance of the villagers bore fruit. A dense forest of *sal* trees became the distinguishing feature of our village – among the neighbouring villages.

Later on, after many years of drudgery and toil in our farm – as the pension of the army was inadequate to raise a family even during those inexpensive days – to eke out a living off the traditional agriculture, my father decided to permanently shift and get settled in a neighbouring business town.

He had realised the potential of commerce to bring prosperity to one after he undertook a few small-time, seasonal businesses in the village, mostly in agricultural products.

There he started a small business in the town. Thankfully, it took-off well and within a couple of years he built his own house in the town.

My father, however, had his roots firmly in the village, where he was born and grew up. He always kept track of the happenings in village and its politics. He went there often to meet his old pals.

Soon he was elated to know that foreign volunteers came to our village along with the District Forest Officer (DFO), on learning about the flourishing sal forest there.

The government authorities, deeply impressed by the efforts of the people of our village to protect the sal forest, decided to further consolidate it.

They began by declaring formally that sal forest as a protected area of the government. The idea of community-forestry has taken roots at the official level by now, with the technical know-how and other input of the foreign volunteers.

The DFO office then implanted nearly twenty thousand saplings of high quality *sal* in that area after growing them at a nursery they hired from my dad.

In fact, one of our 'khet' or farm near the *sal* forest had a good water supply through a small canal built by my father. He grew there tobacco and other such crops which needed adequate irrigation.

The forest officials hired that *khet* as a nursery from us, to locally grow the saplings.

These days, after many years of the governmental

protection, through the practice community forestry, which my dad practiced many decades before it occurred to the authorities, the forest of sal trees has grown even more green and dense near our village.

No one dares to go there alone even during the day, fearing the wild animals, and no one is allowed to cut trees from there even today.

It is a different matter though, that the people from the District Forest Office come there twice every year to clear the forest of unwanted, dried and fallen wood. That wood is used by all the villagers as firewood. Thankfully, it always suffices for their needs throughout the year.

Also, nearly a hundred trees of *'Chyuri'* have also grown in the protected area on their own. A lot of villagers go there during the spring to collect the nectar of the *chyuri* flowers. With this nectar they prepare the *'Chyuri ko Gur'* – a fragrant and sugary delicacy of the area, deeply cherished by the natives and the people elsewhere – which sells at a premium cost.

Conflicts Within and Without

Was the conflict with out an extension of the one with in or was it the other way?

The inertia of the night so totally took control of me that it rendered a day impossible to look up to. It could not be avoided. The pressure was intense but familiar. Looking back it could be imagined how the things might turn out. But there are occasional surprises, pleasant or unpleasant.

Living a day just like the previous one was a difficult prospect. But was there an escape? Weather reflected the mood on an impossibly long day of a summer – when you longed for shorter days of winter – which left you enraged for your inability to control the intensity of light.

The brightness, at times, could be felt getting into the nerves and possess you completely. The day altered between the gloom of rainless clouds overtaking the sun and the sun defeating the clouds to brighten the things again.

The drizzle persisted without yielding any real— rain. Sun turned it into a hot vapour, rising from a barely wet land.

It could be felt on the perspiring skin under the heat of the sun. One felt if this dual heat from above and below will sqeeze every drop of life out of one.

The occasional brightness added to the confusion and irritation. This competition of the sun and clouds took its toll on the body and soul, leaving one unable to decide what was in store just a few moments ahead.

As heat drained the vigour through the pores of the body—the conflict of the heart grew and the confusion of the fickle mind compounded.

The activity to fill the day had to be undertaken. Slowly the pace had to be adjusted to make the life bearable, after the start had been made. If it is too quick it could not be sustained. And if it is too slow it may leave one feeling at a perpetual loss.

The balance appeared ever elusive. Maybe through practice it could be discovered, undertaking which every day is a difficult process.

The oppressive light and mood of the day could not be denied; it had to be answered: But how?

The time has not stopped due to the inability of one to decide about the matters. Maybe there is nothing important, for one, to decide about. Or the things would go on on their own, irrespective of the decisions one made about them. There are people said to be in control of the things, however. They are even said to control the lives of others. But how is that possible? Maybe they thought they were in control, until they were surprised by something.

A life can not be lived always adjusting oneself to others pace. After all, different lives have different directions and the pace suitable for one may be not so for other.

If so, how many directions could there possibly be? Could they all be mapped? What happens when they make the people meet on their way? Maybe making a journey is important. Reaching a destination could be a matter of opinion.

....

Thankfully, it is about evening now. The light of day will soon disappear, and the dark will prevail. One may now be in control of the light at least, to put it off before it gets into one's the nerves. The mood of the weather will be difficult to read and shall cease to cause concern. The rain will announce itself by its sound and its absence could be ignored.

Quiet will replace chaos and echos of the past sounds will fill the mind. The pressure to undertake some activity to fill the time will not be there. The chain of thoughts will be broken by sleep. There could be dreams — good or bad. They can be forgotten or recalled as per the convenience.

Or there could be things happening during the night which could not have been predicted. They can not bother you much as such thoughts could be put-off like the light.

The night will hopefully recharge the energies and hope, needed to face another day. A day thus lived will become a memory to cherish in the times ahead. Was it all some kind of an unyielding romance? But what could be the alternative?

East Meets the West

She had to sit on the ground like some others, though there were enough chairs for everybody present to sit on.

The 'Italian-grass' was grown on the ground. It does not grow sparsely like others and was soft to touch. It gave an impression of a carpet if cut carefully.

The 'Italian-grass' was grown and harvested in square-feet, along with its roots as well; from where it a farmer grew it. The patches were folded like a carpet and transported to be grafted--by the square feet-- on the newer grounds of its buyer.

That austere type of lunch party had a cheerful-ambience on a day when the cold-wind had rendered the winter sun ineffective. It could not put-off the festive mood of the people attending, however.

Many pairs of the eyes returned to her back often, which revealed the split of her bottom and some ample hips on which she was sitting upon. Her trousers were cut small and tight and tied much lower than usual.

The fleshy, white hips were not sun-burnt, like the skin of her face. The very brief underwear was visible which she was wearing, with a sticker declaring the manufacturer of it, very boldly indeed.

The thin cotton T-shirt she was wearing suggested there was no under-cloth below it. The nipples were conspicuous on her not so ample breasts below the shirt.

Below her big, black, plastic-framed glasses, the somewhat square-jaws hinted at a toughness, in spite of the playful smile on her lips.

When she stretched forward, as she did often, a big tattoo of Hindu religious sign 'Om' in multiple colours got revealed on her back, just above the split of her hips. On her straightening the 'Om' disappeared under her T-shirt.

The eyes naughtily returned, looking for the 'Om' and more, lingering on her back, waiting for her to stretch forward again.

She was aware of the attention she was getting, and apparently enjoying it, though she tried to pull the T-shirt lower, occasionally, discreetly slipping her hand behind, while looking at her surroundings, returning a few of the spontaneous smiles, while the eyes met.

She left her seat on the ground, at times, and the T-shirt touched her low-cut trousers – covering everything.

When she stretched backwards, her pelvic bones were partially seen, and her groin had the stretch-marks of pregnancy, though her breast did not suggest if she had ever breast-fed a child. The area around her naval had a tattoo too, and a piercing on it, marked by a glittering top.

She was from a Nordic nation, and a qualified primary school teacher. Her mother was raising her infant daughter at home, while she was away. She had parted with her 'partner' who was the father of her daughter. It was something she had arranged with difficulty.

She was here to have a cultural-experience of the East, for a few months. She liked the culture very much, and the wonderful-people here were simply great. She did not like the creeping modernity into this culture, and wanted it to be preserved like something in a museum, which she wanted to see, on her return here—every time.

She had no idea if and when she would come here again, she told – after she apologetically said she had to return in two months time. When I complimented her on her good English, she said it was poor, while she was studying it at school – refusing to accept it. The brief conversation I tried to make with her did not make her comfortable and she excused herself to return to take her seat on the ground.

I thought I got a hint of what the culture would be like ahead, when the East meets the West.

The Untied Knot
and Haridwar Temple

The appearance of new shoots in the trees on his walk in the morning sun reminded Pravin of yet another spring arriving. It also reminded him that both his sons have not come to see him for the past three years now. He felt older with every passing day.

He had fallen into a routine of waking up early to have a bath and offer prayers in front of the pictures of deities he had established near his bed.

His first and the only surviving wife had recently crossed the age of seventy. Pravin was five years older to her.

After prayer he had many cups of weak tea whilst sitting near the heater of coal he had lit. The hetaer had the remains of the fire after it was used to heat water for his bath and that of his wife and to prepare the tea.

After tea Pravin opened his shop downstairs of his house which he had been operating for the last forty years.

His sons often warned him not to have bath on winter mornings – when they came home on leaves or in the letters they wrote--else he could catch pneumonia. But he did not pay much heed and never caught pneumonia either.

The bath and prayer in the morning left him feeling redeemed and happy, in a way his sons could not understand. His shop did a brisk business before but he now was no more interested in business, as his sons sent him enough money for his meagre expenses – and Pravin had his pension too, from his retirement from the army.

He opened his shop out of habit in early morning. He knew that there were no customers he could expect then. They mostly came from the neighboring villsges and reached the town only by noon.

He liked to meet and chat with his customers. Their children or relations sent letters or money-orders through the post-office from the cities where they worked, in his care. The postman did not visit the villages to deliver the same to them directly.

They collected the letters or money from him and then purchased a few things of daily need from his shop occasionally. Sometimes on credit too, if they received only letters instead of a money-order.

They paid the money in their next visit when they received the money-order finally.

Even if they did not purchase anything from his shop, which offered a lesser variety of goods with the passing years, he never minded. He was happy to just talk about his sons and the children of the people visiting him.

The town abounded with the shop-keeping people of a late middle-age or later, as most of the younger generation of it has migrated to different cities finding that their chances of making a living in the town have become increasingly unlikely.

So the shop keepers too met at each-others' shop and talked to while away the time if they did not have customers at their own shop. It was the case most of the time after a bit busy afternoon, as most customers to those shops returned home by evening.

After opening his shop he cleaned it with a broom made of tall grainy grass. The broom initially dropped more litter than it swept.

He then went for a morning walk. He took along with him his third son Sanju, the only one from his surviving wife, who was a mentally invalid one.

Sanju was in his late twenties already but had a brain of an infant, and rapidly gained weight, if he did not take him for walks for a few days.

He ate so much that he had to stop him being fed by his mother, as he had fallen ill on a few occasions due to over-eating.

Pravin trained him earlier, putting a lot of efforts, to clean his body and brush his teeth. Due to anger and pity, and an asthma that troubled him since his childhood, he could barely control his breathlessness while shouting instructions to his third son to clean himself properly.

Sanju smiled and tried to mock him, taking the whole exercise for a play. At times he slapped him for his insincerity. But then his heart became heavy with pity at his son's invalidity. Pravin regretted for a long time afterwards his rudeness towards his son.

His increasing age lately has left him incapable of following-up with Sanju. His mother intervened often to help her son to even clean his body.

It made an embarrassing scene if there was a visitor seeing them. They did not entertain others except close family members at home now due to their age and the need of privacy for their son.

His wife talked affectionately to her son while brushing his teeth, as if he was still an infant, though he towered over both of his parents. She had intervened while he was himself brushing them, taking away the brush from him. He was full of rage and wanted to pull his wife away from his son. But he felt his breath getting shorter due to his anger. He tried to relax and took a few deep breaths.

Pravin then felt helpless to stop his wife and pitied both of them in his heart — thinking how an invalid child consumes the energies and emotions of his parents so totally.

Soon Sanju forgot all the trainings of cleaning he had received from his father, and waited for his mother to brush his teeth or wash his face or body every time.

At times he got frustrated and shouted at his wife for making their son totally dependent on her even for feeding and cleaning. Pravin asked her who would look after him the way she did after her. But his wife ignored his question and continued with her ways.

In his heart he too had a deep affection for his invalid son. Every time he prayed in front of the deities he wished that somehow his son would recover and become normal like his other two sons. They were born to his other wife. After their mother died when they very too young his first wife started living with them and gave birth to her invalid son.

Pravin had taken his invalid son to many saints and astrologers in the hope that they would some how magically heal him. Also, he had tried his best to get his invalidity treated through doctors practicing either Ayurveda or 'English' medicines.

Things did not improve even a bit in spite of the years past. But he never gave up the hope. He worried a great deal for what would happen to his invalid son after he and his wife were dead. He felt at times guilty for burdening his other two sons, who were doing jobs in the distant cities for their survival and raising their families, with their mentally invalid half-brother.

Pravin often used to ask them when they were home on leave or in the letters he wrote them, if they would take care of their step brother after him. It was just to elicit reassuring words from them. They tried to give him their sincere assurances in this matter.

Their assurances could not satisfy him however, and he tried his best to find a wife for Sanju.

He soon discovered that even the poor people of his caste declined marrying-off their daughter to his third son, including those who had many girls to marry.

He had not lost heart however, and was always trying towards this purpose. To nearly every relation of him he has sent a message to find a bride for Sanju. But there were no replies.

He thought that only his wife would take care of his invalid son and not his stepbrothers.

He also knew that his army-pension would be inherited by Sanju due to his invalidity--after his mother too passed away. There was enough inherited property to raise his family, if, in spite of his invalidity, he got a bride who was industrious and faithful.

In this hope he undertook the 'thread-ceremony' of Sanju. It was well-attended by the people of the town.

Only after a thread-ceremony a man is considered eligible to undertake all the Hindu rituals including the funeral of his parents. It was something he did in the hope of finding him a bride to marry. Also, he thought that his third son will do the final-rites if he or his wife passed-away in the absence of his other two sons, by putting on fire their funeral-pyre.

It was the duty of a son – not a daughter – with a sacred thread around his neck, as was prescribed in the religious books.

His wife often would press him for finding a girl for Sanju's marriage. She herself had asked the relations at her *maiti* to look for a bride for her son.

They both knew that time was passing away for a duty they were not able to fulfill in spite of their hard efforts. Sanju was the centre of the purpose of their daily life for many years now, as they had nothing else to do.

Feeding and cleaning him was what the mother did every day, and entertaining him by continuously talking optimistically to him was what the father did, though the son had a very poor intelligence to understand what he was being told, let alone reply anything.

It was how Pravin controlled the grief of his heart as well, for there was nothing else he could do to help his son. A thin thread of hope bound them together and made the days passable for many years now.

His wife at times lost the patience and cursed her son for being a burden on everybody, while cleaning or feeding him. The father protested to it and talked in reassuring words to his son and his wife. Sometimes it was he who lost the patience and his wife came to the rescue of her son from the unkind words from his father.

The son had acquired a few words from others that – when he uttered them – distracted the attention from him and made others laugh. He used them in such tense situations.

Sanju laughed seeing other people laugh at what he had said.

Pravin often said to his wife that due to his invalidity only their son was with them. Else he too would have gone away to a city to make a living, like his stepbrothers. And they might have been left with nobody to even talk to. It was though only to pacify their increasing frustration about their son that they talked such things.

In spite of his invalidity their son was capable of imitating a few gesture as well if trained and provoked by others. Sanju often touched his nostril with his index finger where the Hindu girls pierce on the left side, asking where his wife was to his parents, indicating at the wives of his stepbrothers in the photographs hanging on the wall.

It was actually something he was made to learn by a few married pals of his younger days, in the neighbourhood. Sanju repeated those gestures in front of his parents and visitors only to create a comical scene and make others distracted from paying attention to him. He probably was uncomfortable of all the pity he received from others for his invalidity deep in his heart in spite of his limited intelligence.

Pravin returned with Sanju to have breakfast which his wife had cooked for them upstairs.

Then they came downstairs to the shop. He read the newspaper and Sanju just waited sitting near him. It was now late morning. If there were visitors at the shop he talked to them and did a business at the shop.

Then it was time for lunch and an afternoon nap upstairs, with the shop closed till afternoon.

He woke up to have the evening tea and opened the shop again. He left the shop to buy vegetables or other essentials in the evening, while Sanju followed him. Often someone engaged Sanju in talks and gesture-making on the way and he was left behind. He was easily distracted. Pravin had to return to disengage him and take him away. Left alone at times some people made Sanju take tobacco or fed him food from an eatery which made him sick for many days. At times someone gave him alcohol to drink and Sanju remained in bed for a few days afterwards. People were hostile to him in some strange ways if he was not protected by Pravin.

By dusk he closed the shop to finally go upstairs. He washed and offered evening prayers. Then he had dinner while watching TV and then went to bed.

He was always surprised at the agility with which his wife cooked three meals a day and evening tea, apart from doing the washing and cleaning.

He rarely saw her not doing anything throughout the day. She was very thin in her small frame and her face had become more wrinkled with the teeth she lost. Now they both were left with only a few molars.

Unlike him however, she was very energetic even at this late age and needed no medication for asthma or high blood pressure like him. At times she lost her appetite due to the gastric problems she had, but was cured as soon she was given a few tablets.

His sons wrote to him often from the city but had not come to see him for some time now. Now he was losing the hope if he would ever see them again.

They wrote reassuring words in their letters but he was becoming restless to see them. Their jobs and families in the city was a matter of satisfaction for him, as some of the youths in his neighbourhood could not finish their studies and remained idle. Many of them became alcoholic when the government made all kinds of liquor readily available in the town. Some of them have died very young, leaving behind young widows and children.

....

During his last visit three years ago Pravin told his elder son how much fondly he wished that he would be taken away on a pilgrimage by his sons.

He told him, for the first time, that he had to untie a knot behind the wall of a temple at Haridwar, the nearest place of pilgrimage.

Pravin told his son that people tied a knot in the shoots of long grass that grew there when they made a wish for something. People returned to untie the knots when their wishes were fulfilled.

Pravin told his son that, even forty years later, the knot he tied there — wishing to father a child — might have been intact.

He further told his son that, in fact, he tied that knot after he married for the third time after his retirment from the army.

"My first wife couldn't raise a single child she bore and delivered as diseases clamied all of them. Then thinking that she was too old to bear another one I married again. My second wife died while giving birth to her first baby. I lost hope by then of being survived by a child.

"I started planting trees in the public places and donated substantially to the charities constructing buildings of a school and or a temple in the neighbouring villages. I did it in the hope that people will remember me for sometime after I pass-away.

"But I knew it well that only children remember their parents lastingly. Then, on advice of an astrologer, I went to Haridwar to make the wish and married for the third time at the age of forty to your mother. Thankfully, I was luckier this time, and was blessed with two sons.

"While raising you and your brother I nearly forgot that I had to fulfil my promise of untying the knot in the grass at the Haridwar temple––for my wish is fulfilled now. Then your mother died and my first wife gave birth to Sanju. I became even more engaged. I even have two grandsons from you now. It is time for me that I went to Haridwar and untied the knot. I think you or your brother should take me there now," Pravin said.

His elder son became irritated to learn this new story about his family. He instead asked, "Did you have a proper medical check-up before marrying my mother?"

Pravin was startled by this question from his elder son. He realised that his son was educated enough to understand these matters and had his own children too. He told, "Only after a proper medical check-up I married for the third time to father you and your brother. You must understand the difficulties I faced while I raised both of you after your mother died young. My first wife helped a great deal in that regard. Her earlier children died because I was away most of the time due to my army job. It was a time ridden with superstitions and a lack of education. A patient with diarrhea was asked to avoid drinking water as it was thought to cause more bouts of it. A large number of young babies in the area died every summer due to the diarrhea alone. When she gave birth to Sanju things became more difficult for me.

"In order to fulfill my wish of having children only I had to marry three times, rather than anything else."

His son looked satisfied with the revelation of these new facts about his family history. Earlier he was not provided with proper facts on asking or got evasive answers to his questions about it. Most of the information about his family he acquired second-hand from an outsider.

It often inadequately explained the multiple marriages of his father, the death of his own mother and the presence of his stepmother and her son in his family. He also recalled that, when he was very young, the father of his mother, when his mother was still alive, went to Haridwar barefoot, walking a distance of more than hundred kilometers.

He returned with the water of the sacred river Ganga again walking barefoot for many days, to undertake a prayer at the temple in his villege with it. Walking barefoot and not using a vehicle during the journey was to not defile the purity of the water. It took him about two weeks to complete this journey.

He did not see his grand-father again, who died after a few years he undertook that journey and prayer.

He said to his father, "I am not able to take you on a pilgrimage of Haridwar this time, as I am running out of leaves from my company. Maybe next time I will try. Or you could go there with my brother when he comes to see you next summer."

Pravin felt a little disappointed on finding his eldest son making such excuses. He expected more understanding and empathy from his eldest son about the tragedies he lived through in his life and the difficulties he faced while fathering and raising his children. And also about his pledge to untie the knot at the temple in Haridwar the indifference of his son was disheartening. Soon his son returned to the city.

Since then already three years have passed and both of his sons have not come to see him.

The last winter he passed with a great difficulty, as his limbs became numb due to cold in mornings and evenings. Also, during the night, it took longer for his body to get warm, after he went to bed, under a load of blankets. Only during the day the sun warmed him a little.

His voice had become unstable these days and at times people couldn't understand what he was saying. He had to repeat himself many times. Also, the business of going downstairs to open the shop and coming up for meals was becoming an increasingly difficult battle for him. He was amazed to think how he did those things effortlessly all those years.

His only solace was the prayers he offered to the deities twice a day. He felt as if all the tumult of his heart calmed for a while after it.

Pravin also tried to take an interest in the TV programs of old cinema songs, in the evenings. He could identify the cine-stars of his time impeccably--to the surprise of his sons, when they were at home--who were dancing to the tunes which were favourite to him.

He often recalled longingly, how many of those cine-stars were dead now. Such thoughts made him nostalgic for the days gone by. Those were the days of his happy and innocent childhood, and then he grew up to join the army to make those journeys to many places. He vividly recalled the different enterprises he undertook to make a living and to raise his family. He smiled often at what a life it had been for him.

Yesterday, when he tried to add sugar to his tea with a spoon, his shaking hand made it with a great difficulty and half of the sugar got spilled near the cup. It brought an ironic smile to his face.

The signs were there that it would be over soon, or so he thought.

The new shoots of spring couldn't lift his sinking heart this morning, though he smiled at the warming sun just to feel distracted and happy. For a moment he thought if he could just pass away without feeling any pain or causing a disturbance to others. There was not much in store for him to look forward to, and he was deeply grateful for having lived a contented and fulfilling life.

But then Sanju, who walking with him, lost his balance and fell on the ground. Cursing him, he lifted him up by his hand and tried to clear the dust from his dress. Sanju smiled his mocking smile and made his utterances – as incomprehensible as ever. "Not yet", the thought came to him clearly. His third son was his unfinished business.

....

Nearly a month ago, his youngest brother had passed-away just a year short of seventy, as he was about to finish his morning bath. He had raised his brother like his own son since his infancy – after their father died early when Pravin was just entering his puberty.

Early death of his father, due to the fall from a chyuri tree, where he went every spring to collect nectar of the flowers, to make a naturally fragrant sugar, was an announcement of the end of his childhood.

Pravin decided to bear the responsibility of looking after his four brothers and two sisters with the help of his grieving young mother – as he was the eldest son.

He went away to look for a living outside his family and village, barely in his teens, though already married to his surviving wife. His wife was just ten years old then.

With two other boys of his age he left the village on one day to look for a job in the wide world about which he knew little as he had never left his village before, without informing his mother. He came to know later that his mother stood on the road outside their house and wept for him for many days after he left.

But it was how people left their home during those times, to try their luck outside their home.

Fortunately he and his friends got recruited in the army, as the war was raging in Europe and the rest of the world, about which they had a little idea.

He sent his first money-order and letter back home, confirming his well--being soon, as soon he got his first salary.

He came home on his first leave two years later, walking for three days from the nearest railway station. He served in the army for almost twenty years before he retired, though the war had ended soon after he joined the army. Life always remained a crisis for him and he tried his best to manage it.

His youngest brother he loved very much, who always remained a timid infant to him after they lost their father. Towards his other brothers and sisters he could not develop the similar kind of feelings.

Pravin had many happy memories of his childhood, while he tried to provide his youngest brother a fatherly love.

He remembered how he took him to cross a village on the way to his school, during his leaves from the army, where there was a notorious dog that chased the children on the way to their school or home.

He tried to teach his brother how not to be afraid of such dogs and walk confidently while ignoring their bark. He told him that dogs identified the people who were afraid of them and they only chased them.

But his youngest brother never learned the trick. Only during his leaves he went to the school. His death saddened him profoundly.

Pravin at times wondered how many tragedies he saw in his life. He recalled that his sons did not come to express their condolence on the demise of his brother.

It never occurred to him that his sons, who he fathered and raised with so many hopes and efforts, would leave him behind like they did.

They too had to make a living for them and their families — he thought, to reassure himself. He was worried if he would be able to keep his promise to the almighty, of untying the knot at Haridwar Temple.

Homework and the Beauty Queen

Avoiding homework costs dearly in the long run, indeed.

In fact, whether it is signing the wrong treaties with the friendly neighbours or the failed peace talks with the rebels, the lack of proper homework on the part of authorities is often underlined by the learned people of the society.

I do not worry much these days, when I see my young son distressed by the anxiety of his homework when he returns from the school, or during his festival holidays. It is another matter that he has barely completed four years of his life and is in his second year at the school.

Concerned about his homework, which I considered disproportionate – like the assets of a bureaucrat, to his known source of income – to his age, I talked before to his teacher about it.

She stood her puritanical ground firmly on this matter and insisted that – right from the beginning – the children must develop the habit of doing their homework, lest they end up becoming a failure in their later years – like the people occupying the responsible positions in the country. Convinced fully, I gave up my doubts.

What vexes me most is that the homework of my son demands my continuous attention to be accomplished. It disturbs my few moments of leisure and solitude in the evenings, as if my son's homework was intended for me as a punishment for escaping my own during my school years.

This year's Miss Nepal contest was remarkable for many reasons. First because a group led by a popular left-leaning intellectual-columnist Khagendra Sangraula vandalized and burnt the gate at the venue, erected by the organisers.

It was a contention of the columnist that a village-woman who endlessly toils to make the ends meet and manages her alcoholic husband as well is the real beauty queen of Nepal.

Maybe he is right and we can ignore these catwalking, matchstick-figured beauty queens, who practice looking good and talking glibly for the better part of the year. They do not represent the women of Nepal perhaps.

This year's beauty contest was more important for the fact that it had a former bureaucrat as its chief judge. He finally asked the ineluctable and hackneyed question: 'What would you do if you become the Prime Minister of the nation?'

Indeed, it was a question you feared most during your school-days and became dumbfounded whenever faced by it. Even during those days the brightest students produced the best answers to this question.

To my surprise, the girl, who answered best this question, won the crown of the beauty queen finally, as also was pointed out by the wise commentators, later on, in their newspaper columns.

Indeed, if a former bureaucrat – if not a headmaster – is around as the chief judge, it may cost one the crown of a beauty queen – if one did not anticipate this question and do the proper homework, to answer it.

Though, as the only originality of the event, the Nepalese beauty-queen this year pushed away the first-runner up of the contest, who came ahead to greet her with a kiss when her victory was announced; and the second runner up threw away the bouquet presented to her by the organisers, before she started crying – accusing the organizers of being unfair and biased towards her. There was nothing of a love-lost type of situation here, like among the Madonna and Britney Spears.

Surely, this year's beauty-queen must have been prompt to do her homework during her school-days too. It was smart of her to offer the perfect answer to a question rarely expected in a beauty contest. Also, as very few of the beauty contestants retain the hope to become the PM of the nation, unlike a bureaucrat, and mostly end up gyrating their pelvis in a video-music album, or in a movie.

Though they do not tire of reiterating their

commitment to the social services, during the contest; taking it for granted that there will be victims needing their charity too, in the society. This pastime was considered of only the royals before. Now, in the absence of royalty, everybody with any claim to fame or fortune talks about devoting his/her life to the cause of charity. Middle-class people's fantasies and idesyncracies never cease to amuse one.

One wonders if this year's beauty-queen would have won herself a job in the bureaucracy too, if she were being interviewed for one — instead of a beauty crown — on account of her answer to a question which proved to be the *piece de resistance* of the contest, as per the wise columnists.

Ingenuous imitation of foreign trends, backed up by domestic business interests, create an unintended mimicry, to the delight of a bemused onlookers, and provoke disingenuous protests as well. In which the intellectuals and writers end up burning things or pelting stones.

The Crackling Bank Notes

A few days ago he got the information that his salary of the last three months has come at the District Education Office.

He did not go to receive it immediately as he had to finish *ropain* (rice-plantation), before it stopped raining. He was a headmaster at a primary school in a nondescript village with no other staff.

The school was situated two miles away from the village, where very young children could not go every day due to the distance. Next to it was a steep hill and the rice fields in the small valley below the hill.

Those fields were irrigated by a canal built by the villagers by the water from a fall at the eastern end of the valley. Also, there was a watermill to crush the grains to make flour. It was powered by the water from the fall. The water flew through the valley to the west to the big river Mahakali a mile away from the valley.

Next to the valley there was an equally steep climb and a thick forest before one approached another nondescript village at the top of the climb.

Obviously, the headmaster had to look-after every job at the school as he was the only employee there.

For the past few weeks however, due to the *ropain*, he had left the school to the care of one of his cousins.

His cousin had failed in the last year's School Leaving Certificate exam and was free until the another exam next spring. He – since he was a student – rarely contributed in the daily domestic chores or agricultural work of the family, and was a late riser. By the time his cousin reached the school it was already a mid-day. The children were already tired of playing noisily by then.

The bell was there to announce the beginning and the end of a school-day, but no one rang it. His cousin did not believe in interfering in the things the students did. The students, in turn, also left him alone.

Around three pm the children ran away from the school again making a lot of noise on their way back to the nondescript village.

The headmaster had finally finished his *ropain*. The rain was good this year and he expected a good harvest at the beginning of festivals when autumn begun.

He prepared the details of his attendance at the school for the past three months to submit to the District Education Office before drawing his salary. He signed it before he put the seal of the school on it.

On that morning he left for the district headquater which was two hours climb away from the village, leaving the school to his cousin once again.

He got his three months' salary as one bundle of the blue-coloured fifty rupee notes, another bundle of the brown ten rupee notes and a third bundle of the smaller, red-coloured, five rupee notes, and a few coins as well.

All three bundles were of brand new, crackling bank notes which were recently issued by the central reserve bank in the capital. Their serial numbers from one to hundred were intact.

He wondered sometimes if the government always printed new notes to pay for the salaries of its employees every three-month.

He stuffed those bundles in his pockets of the coat which he wore only when he came to the district headquarter or to attended an important ceremony in the village, like a marriage or a religious ceremony.

Then he went to a food stall with thatched roof. There were dirty tables and stools to sit on in it. The utensils were spread on its earthen floor.

He ordered a glass of local wine and a plate of fried fish. The fish was fresh since the river was near the town, but the wine was bitter and coarse. All the packed food available in the town was stale and damp though, as the town did not yet have roads and fresh supplies of goods to it were irregular on the back of mules.

He noticed a few of his fellow villagers

approaching the stall. They were the ones who came to the town almost every day. Some of them sold milk or vegetables they produced, and others simply because they had nothing else to do.

Almost everybody who came to the town returned home drunk in the evening. The villagers sold fresh milk and vegetables after walking uphill for two hours only to drink the cheap home-made liquor with the money they had earned. They mostly returned home empty handed in the evening. Many of them died young due to alcoholism.

Some of the villagers coming to the town were caught and sent to the prison by the police more recently, as a drug called *Attar* was recovered from them.

Attar was called Hashish by the officials. Actually it was a centuries-old practice for the villagers to rub the cannabis leaves in their hands during their leisure and than rub the hands hard together to collect the black colored *Attar*.

First it appeared as small pin like soft pieces. Then it grew thicker as the hands were rubbed more. It finally gained the thickness of a thin thread and was ready.

The threads of *attar* were stored weaved together like a rope and they got harder as they dried. The villagers either sold or consumed it, smoking it with tobacco in a clay-pipe or in a cigarette. It was to amuse themselves after a day's hard work. The government authorities had a tolerant attitude towards this practice earlier and one heard that there were centers in the capital of the country where it was sold and tourists came from world over to smoke the *attar* of Nepal.

But, more recently, the government had become very strict about the people producing or dealing in Hashish. Some of the villagers never knew that what was done for centuries in their homes had become a serious crime now.

Only when they were apprehended by the police while they were trying to sell the *attar* in the town that they realized that they were dealing in an illegal trade.

So the dealings of *attar* got reduced in the town and the business went underground. But it never got eliminated as there was a demand for it.

Among the peasants, who could not afford the heavily taxed alcohol distributed by the government-approved shops or liked alcohol; smoking *attar* was a cheap and easily available indulgence to amuse themselves.

Also, since in the mythological stories Lord Shiva was said to consume it routinely, *attar* was not as stigmatized as alcohol in the villages. There was a town named *attria* because it was a trading center of *attar* earlier, in the neighborhood.

After it became a contra banned item its cost increased. Every time it reached a bigger town its cost inflated severely. In big towns the rules of the government were more rigorously implemented and the people—who had many other kinds of amusement available to them, and their life was physically less hard too than in villages of the country—seemed to prefer *attar* for some strange reasons, though it did cost much higher than alcohol. Criminalized and stigmatized, *attar* or Hashish was as popular as ever.

On many instances the police came to a village from a town to destroy the cannabis plants growing there in the wilderness. But it was an enormous task and they had a little patience, as they had to return by the evening. If it was a symbol to create awareness among the villagers about the criminality related to this plant it seemed to have not convinced the villagers. As they continued to use it as before after the police returned.

....

The headmaster knew that his fellow-villagers had come to the stall well-aware that he was there with his salary in his pocket. He ignored them for some time while they repeatedly smiled at him to catch his attention.

Later he asked them to join him, after a few more drinks he had. Bonhomie returned to the desolate looking stall, as everyone was talking loudly and laughing – while sipping the coarse wine and munching the fried fish.

The headmaster suddenly started vomiting and passed-out. He lay unconscious on the earthen-floor, under the dirty table he was drinking upon. His clothes were soaked in the foul-smelling things he had vomited. His fellow villagers did not touch him, and left silently, one-by-one, after finishing their drinks.

The owner of the stall too did not touch the unconscious headmaster. He witnessed such scenes almost every day when the government employees who were erstwhile peasants mostly--not much different from the ones who came to sell the fresh milk and vegetables-- visited the town to collect their salaries.

The stall-owner was always surprised to see that mostly the person paying for the drinks passed-out instead of the ones who drank it free.

He knew that the headmaster would be fine after a few hours. By the afternoon the headmaster had regained his consciousness. He paid the bills presented by the stall-owner from the new crackling bank notes. The fluid he vomited on his dress has dried up as the day of the summer was hot. He dusted himself and washed his face before he left the stall and went towards the shops of the town.

He knew that it could be another three-months before he came to the town to receive his salary again. So he did a little shopping as well. He bought things like sugar, tea-leaves, tobacco and biscuits.

He also purchased a few candies for his two daughters and a big coconut for his wife.

His wife has asked him to buy her a sari before he left his home in the morning, as she did always. The headmaster had managed to appease her with a big coconut every time.

He purchased new clothes for his family only when he got a double salary before the *dashain* festival every year.

By dusk he proceeded to the crossing from where he had to return home. There he met all his fellow-villagers who had enjoyed his drinks and food earlier but abandoned him when he passed-out.

They smiled at him and made excuses for leaving him unconscious at the stall. The headmaster did not mind and ignored them.

Since he felt very weak to walk back home the headmaster hired a mule which one of his fellow-villagers operated to ferry goods or the people—old or young, sick or healthy, men or women—who could afford his mule to hire. Any other kind of transportation was not yet available in the town.

The mule operators in the town came to the town every morning and returned home every evening.

The headmaster rode the mule and his goods in a bag were loaded on the shoulders of the mule-owner. Along with the other villagers returning home on foot—it looked like a caravan moving on that moon lit evening. It was a cool evening filled with the sweet smell of pine forest through which they were passing. They were descending the hill to reach the plateau where their village was situated.

Some people were talking loudly while others walked in silence. A day was over with its highs and lows.

In the next two weeks the headmaster had done away with his three months' salary. He returned the money he had borrowed from the villagers during the months he went without a salary.

He had the local wine – available, illegally, also in the village, but only after paying a little extra cost – on a few more evenings, with some of his friends.

He once also visited the only prostitute of the area in the neighbouring village, who also moonlighted as a cleaner in the famous temple of that village.

The headmaster took his turn among the crowd of her clients who were mostly the people who did jobs in the cities and were home on leaves.

Almost everyone in the queue knew each other. A few of them even exchanged pleasantries, while waiting for their turn. A few of them said that they had condoms with them, particularly the ones who were on leaves from their city jobs, but most others had none like the headmaster.

During those two weeks the headmaster made every payment from the new bank-notes of his salary. He was always aware through the serial numbers how much exactly he was left with.

In fact, the fellow villagers too noticed those crackling bank notes while they did the rounds among them. A few villagers joked about the notes with the headmaster, saying that they had seen the prostitute of the area shopping with them at a shop in the neighbouring village. The headmaster smiled on it and ignored the matter.

Drinking alcohol, returning home on a mule or visiting a prostitute separated him from the common peasants of his village, who were penniless mostly. He was proud of his job and the salary he earned.

At times even the bemused headmaster received those new notes back from others as change. After a few weeks however, his crackling bank notes disappeared from the village. No one was sure whether they got dirty in the hands of villagers so quickly, or returned to the town from where they came.

Introduction

"Worrying about your debts is foolish when the nation itself is deep into debts, be it Nepal or India...," said an uncle once.

He had a large progeny which multiplied with abandon to make sure that the crises in his life remained permanent. He, on occasions, grew a beard to become a Sadhu to leave home to avoid the moneylenders visiting him to recover their loans.

But the uncle always returned clean-shaved after he made some money in an unknown enterprise at an unknown place. He left again in his beard some time later, when again the things became unmanageable at his home.

An educated cousin once quoted in Sanskrit and then translated that one should '... drink ghee-- (symbolically meaning lead a lavish life)--even by borrowing money.'

Surprisingly, it is reported that people across the world mostly do not mind living on credit nowadays. After all, human existence entails some privileges that could be paid for later, or so one might be prompted to think.

Having been born in 1966, life was generally secure and stable, except that the author lost his mother too early. But the security was on borrowed finances which had to be paid later.

The school education mostly in India, and then in Kathmandu, at times subsidized in small portions by the scholarships this author won, did not tell how the world works. And finding it contrary to what was assumed was another shock.

After working since he completed his teens, for his living and raising a family, later; after the loans were paid first; earlier in a department of the then His Majesty's Government--where he got a hundred rupees' raise in his salary on the King's birthday--a raise which also caused an increase in the house-rent he paid and in the cost of the goods of daily necessity--and then in different corporate jobs, part owning and abandoning a retailing business in the meanwhile, when money started to disappear on the face of depleting inventories; a situation which appeared like building into a dispute among the partners--this author has discovered how little could be taken for granted.

A lot of the conventional wisdom, the kind which persists here, has to be set aside towards that end.

It had been a long apprenticeship however, just to discover his philosophy of life, which is not of much use when applied to deal with the real situations. As they normally are backed up by too many hidden, complex issues and the underlying psychological energies of the various invisible people involved.

Defining alone such arrangements could consume a lifetime, let alone be solving anything.

I recall having witnessed a middle-aged, disheveled person leaving Kathmandu on one cold morning of a winter, with a typical peasant's bag on his back.

He was shouting out loudly in the street that life in Kathmandu city was not easy and he shall never return. He was trying to make an eye-contact with anybody who looked at him, expecting words of sympathy perhaps--if nothing more.

But the people, most of them on their morning walk--or a few other men carrying fresh vegetables in bright colours from the villages in the vicinity of the city in two baskets; one in front and another on their back--hanging by ropes from a stick on their shoulders; their backs crooked to balance the load giving a strange, feminine, distressed and grotesque rhythm to their hurried steps as they walked; while the low-cloud reduced the visibility to make everybody around look mysterious-- looked at him for once and then they looked away, as if they did not hear him. He was not insane but was very agitated.

It happened a long time ago. What was to follow was a--then widely underestimated--armed-leftist revolution, a few years after the establishment of democracy. The democracy came after an earlier political movement, which curtailed the power of monarchy scantily. It was not enough however, and people wanted something more substantial.

The leftist revolution was limited to the countryside in the start. It spread widely and quickly and nearly turned into a civil war. It put the urban areas too under a perpetual siege.

This situation persisted for more than a decade consuming tens of thousands of lives.

When the underground leadership of the revolution became public, after the political agreements between the establishment and the rebels allegedly were reached in a foreign language and soil, they first appeared wearing suits and ties and were invariably over-weight. Besides they all wore hats of different style which gave them a comical look.

They looked more like executives of a multinational company instead of the rugged guerrilla fighters of the Che Guevara kind. To this day they continue to surprise one by their atrocious dress sense. The strange color combination of their suits and ties, which they invariably wear in public even now--when many of them have already occupied many responsible positions in the government--instead of the Nepalese national dress like other politicians, still makes one smile.

Their proposed solutions to the problems of the people of the country are equally strange.

Most of them though ride the most exclusive imported automobiles and wear Swiss-made wrist watches these days besides many rings in their fingers. Those rings are actually charms which a spiritual Guru gives to his followers who need an incredible amount of luck to succeed in their professions.

In the meanwhile the BBC radio—so trusted before by the people for bringing them reliable news--had already withdrawn and apologized for a debate, which it could not conduct in any case, due to the overwhelming protests of the Nepalese people. The topic of the debate was if Nepal has failed as a nation and it should join its southern country's union as recourse.

Then there was the carnage in the Royal palace which eliminated the King and the most of his immediate family. Consequently, among others, there were changes, which have not stopped until this day, in the school textbooks of my sons, often during midway of an educational year.

By their own hands and as per the instructions of a teacher they were asked to cancel a printed text and replace it with another by writing it themselves. It was about the history and the contents of the country that things were becoming irrelevant fast. When they asked me for explanations I was at a loss.

Life has altered irrevocably meanwhile, though the things look less than settled. The violence during the revolution was shocking and deeply disturbing, as it never manifested itself before otherwise. Or it was not reported perhaps, though the distress was ubiquitous, waiting for just a spark to blow up the things.

Developing a habit of reading and writing offered one a great opportunity to attempt at comprehending the things around. A nervous energy could be felt behind the work presented here, as it may seem, rather than a conviction of any sort.

However, there was no other way to cope with the anxiety and uncertainty for this author, of the times he lived in. Hopefully, some of the stories in this book explain the matters and the rest is an attempt to recall the times and the people who always have remained in one's head over the years and decades, as they could not be explained fully. Obviously, nothing ever concludes.

(July 26, 2007)

To my wife Sushma